Walter
I hope you
enjoy my book!
Best regards
Ste A. Fulco
4-8-22

# MICKEY MANTLE'S

## LAST HOME RUN

STEVEN A. FALCO

# MICKEY MANTLE'S LAST HOME RUN

*Certain characters in this work are historical figures, and certain events portrayed did take place. However, this is a work of fiction. All of the other characters, names, and events as well as all places, incidents, organizations, and dialogue in this novel are either the products of the author's imagination or are used fictitiously.*

*iUniverse books may be ordered through booksellers or by contacting:*

*iUniverse*
*1663 Liberty Drive*
*Bloomington, IN 47403*
*www.iuniverse.com*
*1-800-Authors (1-800-288-4677)*

*ISBN: 978-1-5320-5208-8 (sc)*
*ISBN: 978-1-5320-5209-5 (e)*

*Library of Congress Control Number: 2018911038*

*Print information available on the last page.*

*iUniverse rev. date: 06/12/2019*

*For Martin, Bobby and the Mick
and for George*

# CHAPTER 1

# Number 535

September could be a lousy month for a baseball fan, especially for a baseball fan whose team was twenty games out of first place with only nine games to play. But that was how it was for Yankees fans last September. Even so, I decided I had to go to one more game. I wanted to go with my girlfriend, Maggie, but she had color guard practice or something stupid like that. I knew she didn't really like baseball, but well, I'd kind of hoped she'd make an exception. I knew my friend Frankie was too busy getting into trouble, and my genius friend Phil was too busy studying. My friend Jonathan was noncommittal.

Still, I had to go. I had to go to one more game to see the Mick. Now, I wasn't saying the Mick wouldn't be back in '69. As a matter of fact, I was sure he would be, and he'd probably double his home run production. But I knew I just had to go to one more game.

I'd listened to yesterday's game when I got home from school, and well, I didn't like the way the announcers were talking about the Mick. I mean, yeah, it was great and all that—he hit his 535th home run and surpassed Jimmy Foxx for third place on the all-time home run list. Only Willie Mays and fat old Babe Ruth had hit more home runs than the Mick. The broadcasters said that Denny McClain, the Tiger pitcher, grooved the pitch for the Mick to hit out. After all, the Tigers were winning the game 6–1, they had already clinched the pennant, and McClain was on his way to winning his thirty-first game of the year, which sure as heck was enough wins for anybody. But I didn't even care if Denny McClain grooved the pitch. What really bothered me was how the Tigers fans gave the Mick such an ovation. Heck, no one had to tell me that the Mick was great and deserved an ovation, but they said on the radio that the fans were cheering so much because they thought it might be the Mick's last appearance at Tiger Stadium and that McClain grooved the pitch because McClain, who deep down was really a Mickey Mantle fan, figured the Mick might not have many more opportunities to surpass Jimmy Foxx's record.

I thought the big fuss was all pretty stupid because the Mick would be back next year and maybe he'd even catch up to good old Willie Mays.

Well, I was going, and that was that. It was a nice, warm Friday night. I ate a quick supper and told my parents I would be going to the game with Jonathan and Frankie. Of course, I lied about Frankie, whose interest in baseball seemed to have faded and who was planning to go to some dopey Iron Butterfly concert with Murray and his gang. I only half lied about Jonathan, because

Jonathan had said he wanted to go, but he had to help his father with something, so he'd meet me there. I told him I'd be getting general admission upper-deck seats, and since the crowd probably wouldn't be very big, I'd get a spot behind home plate. I was counting on Jonathan to show up because it would feel a little funny going all the way to Yankee Stadium alone—but I could have belted Jonathan when he said he wanted to go only so he could pay his respects to the Mick. Jonathan said that 1968 was a year when everybody did a lot of respect paying, so he might as well do it for Mick's playing career. That statement made me sick to my stomach. I even called up my brother at college to see if he'd like to take a trip home to see one more game. Now, there was no doubt I would have belted my brother for what he said if he hadn't been seventy-five miles away and on the other end of the phone line.

"So you want to see the great Mickey Mantle one more time before he hangs up his spikes."

*Bam!* My brother would have been missing some teeth if he'd said that to my face. Oh, and besides, my brother was too busy with more important stuff, like burning down the college administration building. Somehow, things were different with my brother those days. In fact, everything was different those days.

I hopped the ole 145 bus at 5:40 and headed on out to New York City. I always liked the bus ride to New York. I liked to gaze out the window and check out the scenery. It was a heck of a lot more interesting than the boring scenery on my family's drives out to Pennsylvania to visit Aunt Tillie. It was amazing how many things I could see on the bus ride to New York City. I liked to check out all the little stores, used-car lots, and cozy houses. A lot of the houses were real close together, and I wondered how people could stand living jammed next to each other. Of course, the best part of the trip was the New Jersey Turnpike. It was fabulous. Seriously. The bus passed by all the factories, with their grimy windows and tall smokestacks. Then there were the junkyards with smashed-in old cars and beat-up yellow school buses all piled on top of each other. I could see it all from the turnpike. There were truck yards with row after row of truck trailers parked but ready for action, and there were railroad yards with tracks leading all over the place. There were junky old freight cars, big black oil cars, and boxcars, just like in my old train set. Then the bus passed by the old Budweiser factory, with its flashing neon sign that changed into an eagle flapping its wings, and of course, there was Newark Airport, with the big, loud jets roaring right over the bus. Then came my favorite sight of all: the Pulaski Skyway. We used to take it when my father took us to Yankees games. I kind of missed riding on it, with its heavy iron railing that seemed to disappear as I peered through it while going fifty miles an hour. From the turnpike, I could see how long the old Pulaski Skyway was and how it spanned the roads, truck yards, and murky river inlets on its way past Jersey City to the Holland Tunnel. It was a real sight. Seriously.

The other thing I liked to do on the bus ride to New York City was just sit and daydream. This time, I couldn't help but think back to last spring. I'd known back then that things were gonna be different. I'd just never expected all the yelling, crying, bleeding, and dying, and I'd never expected to be right in the middle of it.

# CHAPTER 2

# The Mick

As the spring of 1968 began, I knew that year was gonna be different. The previous year, our freshman baseball team was a joke. Our team had a record of one win and seventeen losses—nothing much to be proud of. Sure, we had lots of characters who weren't really JV material, and I didn't expect a lot of them to try out this year. Dionne, our left fielder, went out for the golf team. It was just as well. I mean, he was the only guy I'd ever seen who thought the strike zone was from the shoe tops to the knees. But he was deadly. If a pitcher made a mistake and got one too low to ole Dionne, he'd drive the ball three hundred feet, and boy, could he put a slice on the ball. Reggie, our center fielder, didn't come back either. He said he wanted to stick with a "real" sport: basketball. Reggie thought he was an all-around athlete. He thought he could play baseball, but I thought the real reason he didn't go out for the JV team was because he never lived down the time he tried to make a Willie Mays basket catch of a line drive. Reggie made the catch all right, but he didn't realize that when Willie Mays made his basket catches, they were always swishes, not bank shots. Poor Reggie took the line drive squarely on the chest, and the ball bounced right into his glove. The batter was out, but so was hot dog Reggie for a whole month with a cracked rib.

I was ready. Of course, I hadn't stopped practicing since last season ended. All during the fall, I'd gone to the batting cages in Brookfield, and during the winter, I'd worked out down in the cellar. I knew it would be tough this year. There could be no messing around, and I wanted to be ready. I did the usual garbage exercises, including push-ups and sit-ups, both of which I despised. I'd swing my lead bat about thirty to forty times. I'd also throw my cement balls, which were pretty great. *Maybe I should patent the idea*, I thought. *Sell 'em to the Yankees. Maybe get together with Ellie Howard and sell my cement balls with his batting doughnuts.* Last summer, my father put a patio in the backyard. While he was working, I put some of the cement through the holes in some whiffle balls I had. When they hardened, I had me a few cement balls. I stored them until the winter, and after the first snowstorm, I took out the little gems and went up to the snow-covered field, where I threw them around. I'd throw them as far as I could. It wasn't easy to throw them, but it built up my arm. I was so used to the cement balls that when the season came along, a normal baseball felt like a whiffle ball, and unfortunately, when I started throwing a regular baseball again, it would curve like a stupid whiffle ball. I'd always had some trouble throwing the ball straight anyway.

I was going out for shortstop, but my secret desire was to play center field like the Mick. However, I figured I was better defensively, and if I was going to make the team, I'd have to do it with my glove, unless my hitting made a miraculous improvement. Anyway, the Mick started out as a shortstop. I was going to continue my switch-hitting, even though everybody was telling me I should stick with batting righty. Heck, they were probably right since I could hardly even hit righty, but I was thickheaded. I had always been a switch-hitter. I figured I might as well go down as a switch-hitter. I mean, most of us grew up as switch-hitters. All of us Yankees fans sure did. Back when I was a kid, my friends were divided into Yankees fans and non-Yankees fans, and way out on the outskirts were the ones who didn't even like baseball. If you were a Yankees fan, you had to like the Mick, and since the Mick was a switch-hitter, well, everybody had to try it. Most of us were natural righties, so we'd have to learn to bat lefty. The few guys who were weird enough to be natural lefties had enough trouble learning to hit lefty with any coordination to begin with, so they really didn't try to imitate the Mick.

I always had the best success switch-hitting, probably because I was the most dedicated Mickey Mantle fan in town. Way back when I was four years old, my brother and I would play the Mickey Mantle and Yogi Berra Game. It was just a dopey game in which my brother would pretend he was Yogi Berra, and I'd be the Mick, and we'd whack an old, beat-up tennis ball around the backyard. Since I was the Mick, I'd have to bat lefty and righty. So I guessed I kind of had gotten a head start on everybody, and I guessed that was why I refused to change. I mean, you couldn't just go around changing something you'd been doing for eleven years. I probably started the switch-hitting craze in our town. When I started playing Little League, there I was, imitating the Mick and switch-hitting, so everybody else gave it a try—except for the lefties. Gradually, as I got older, everybody kind of gave up on the idea, except me—and I wasn't about to when we tried out for JV.

I thought the Mick was the greatest. I mean, that was an objective opinion. At fifteen, I probably was a little too old to have baseball players for heroes, but in all honesty, the Mick was the greatest. Seriously. The first Yankees game I ever went to was really a big deal, and heck, it should have been. People made a big deal out of the first day you walked, your first trip to the stupid dentist, your first day of school, and all that kind of crap. Well, as far as I was concerned, none of that even came close to that first day at Yankee Stadium. Oh, and I knew how my father liked to make a big deal out of taking his little kids to the big ballpark in the Bronx. He had to get his kicks about his little fatherly duty. But heck, it was all right with me. I felt sorry for any kid with a father who wouldn't take his kid out to the big ballpark. Anyway, my father played it up rather well. It was a summer afternoon when I was six, and my brother and I were doing—what else?—playing baseball. We had progressed beyond the Mickey Mantle and Yogi Berra Game. We were pretending we were other players, such as Whitey Ford and Hank Bauer. Well, my father arrived home around his usual time, at about four o'clock, so we knew we had about an hour before we'd get the supper call. That was just fine with me because my brother's team was beating mine, and I'd need a few more innings to try to catch up. Well, my father said, "Come on, boys. Let's go. Supper's going to be early tonight."

I was understandably pissed off and threw away my bat since I was behind in our game. My brother, though, was smiling from ear to ear. Not only was he ahead in the score, but it seemed he had a good idea what my father was up to. He bolted to the back door and left me—actually, Hank Bauer—up at the plate with two out and two on in the bottom of the seventh. I started whining and tore after him. I just about tackled him at the back door, and while I was screaming my head off, my father told us to go wash up, as supper would be early. Then we heard my mother ask my father if he was going to call Tony. Well, that did it for my brother. He knew right then because whenever my father was going to a ball game, he'd ask my uncle Tony to come. My brother tore into the house, and I stayed out on the porch, brooding. A few minutes later, my father came over to the screen door and said, "Hey. You know, I hear Whitey Ford's pitching tonight."

I just sat there and pouted.

"Yeah, and I'd sure hate to miss the first inning," he said. "It sure is a long ride over to the stadium. Sure hate to miss Mickey Mantle's first at bat."

Well, that did it. I nearly broke the door down. "We're going to Yankee Stadium?" I yelled.

"We sure are," my dad said, and he picked me up and spun me around while I practiced my best Yankee Stadium cheer. I kind of lost my cool, but what the heck? I was only a little squirt, and that was the biggest day of my life up to that point.

The rest of the night was one big succession of oohs and aahs. *Ooh, the Holland Tunnel is long. Aah, we just passed the borderline into New York.* It was neat to drive through the tunnel and see the little sign for New Jersey on one side and the sign for New York on the other. I always thought that some guy must have painted some kind of yellow line down at the bottom of the Hudson River to divide New Jersey and New York. It was always exciting to pass from one state to another and was especially exciting to do so while at the bottom of a river.

Well, when we got to the stadium, there were more oohs and aahs. Yankee Stadium was positively great. I would still kind of get goose bumps whenever I went there afterward. That evening, when we made our way out from under the grandstand to where we could see the field, it was beautiful—the huge expanse of green grass, the beautiful design of the infield, all those blue seats, and the players down on the field, throwing the balls around in real life. Afterward, the scene still kind of grabbed me whenever I thought about it.

The game was pretty tight. Yogi Berra got a two-run single to put the Yanks ahead in the sixth, which made my brother's day. However, the Mick was doing lousy. He flew out once, then walked, and then struck out twice, which made me want to crawl under my seat.

My uncle Tony was cheering away with glee. Uncle Tony was kind of the oddball in the family. Everybody else, including my father and my other uncles, was a Yankees fan, except Uncle Tony, who was a Brooklyn Dodgers fan and then, unfortunately, a Mets fan. Anyway, Uncle Tony was all right. He was a good baseball fan, except his loyalties were a little messed up. It must have been something in his childhood. My father was an old Joe DiMaggio fan, but he had learned to accept the Mick as Joe D's successor. It was good to know that my dad was there behind me when I really needed him.

Well, the Mick came up in the bottom of the ninth with one on, two out, and the Yanks losing 4–3. He worked the count to three and two, and I was so nervous I could barely watch. Then *bam*! The Mick hit a rocket out to deep right-center field! *Going! Going! It is gone! Holy cow!* The Mick blasted a fastball halfway up the bleachers for a game-winning home run. The whole place went wild! My brother and I jumped around, screaming our heads off. My dad was on his feet, cheering. Some old geezer in the row in front of us spilled his beer on a lady next to him, and she didn't even seem to mind. Poor old Uncle Tony just kind of silently sat back. I figured he wished deep down that he wasn't cursed with such bad luck as to be a Brooklyn Dodgers fan and a Mets fan.

The Yankees won the game 5–4. We left the stadium beaming. We stopped at a crowded souvenir stand, and my father bought my brother and me each a Yankee pennant. We got a package of ten autographed Yankee pictures. I got a Mickey Mantle button, and my brother got a Yogi Berra button. Then we bought a pen-and-pencil set with the Yankee emblem, which we said we were going to give to our mother, but we knew for sure she wouldn't really want it, and we'd eventually get it. We tried to get something for our grandma, but my dad kind of caught on and said we had enough souvenirs. I was pretty tired on the ride back home, but I was still glowing inside. I was snug in the back seat of that big car, with nothing at all to worry about. The Yanks had won, the Mick was a hero, and we had another carefree summer day ahead. I was quiet, and my dad kept turning around to see if we were asleep. My brother could sleep anywhere, so he was out like a light, but I was still wide awake. I was content to gaze out the window and look at the lights of New Jersey twinkling in the Hudson River as we drove down the Westside Highway. I had a picture of Mick's home run swing in my mind, and I was thinking about how tomorrow we'd be out in the backyard, whacking around the old baseball, and I'd try to imitate that beautiful swing. It had been quite a night. Seriously.

# CHAPTER 3

# Frankie

I kept buggin' my friend Frankie to get in shape because this year was gonna be different, but like usual, Frankie could never take anything seriously. "I *am* friggin' in shape," he'd always say. Frankie was my best friend, although sometimes I didn't like to admit it. I used to bug him to go with me to the batting cages, but he always had an excuse. Frankie was one of those people who always had an excuse. But he was such a likeable guy that I could never really get mad at him. Everybody basically liked him because he acted like such a dimwit. I was probably the only person alive who really knew that down deep, Frankie wasn't a dimwit.

He had kind of a tough year last year on our freshman baseball team. He was the fourth-string right fielder. Now, everybody knew that being fourth-string anything wasn't exactly something to be proud of, and in baseball, the worst players were always stuck out in right field because the ball wasn't hit out there too often. So to be fourth-string right fielder, well, that was pretty bad. But actually,

Frankie really wasn't that bad of a fielder. The problem was that he always managed to appear bad in the field. One time in practice, Frankie missed eleven straight fly balls—and when I say "missed," I mean he didn't even get a glove on one of them. The problem was, Frankie was wearing the wrong pair of eyeglasses. He had recently had his glasses changed, but that day, for some reason, the moron brought the wrong pair to practice, so he could hardly see anything. Frankie was also injury prone. He missed half of last season with a sprained finger that he sustained while tying his shoe. Seriously. In the only game he actually started, he was knocked unconscious in the third inning when he ran into the football goalpost while chasing a long foul fly ball. What a dimwit, right?

As far as hitting, well, statistics didn't lie. Frankie was up eight times freshman year, and the only time he got on base was when he was hit by a pitch while trying to bunt. The ball hit him right in the stomach, so he had to leave the game. He sat on the bench for the rest of the game, swaying back and forth and moaning. The seven other times Frankie appeared at the plate, he struck out. He did manage to hit three foul balls. It was sort of sad when the players would sit around and talk about hitting, and Frankie could mention only his three foul balls. But he was still proud of them, even though two were on checked swings. Despite all of that, Frankie always assured me he was going out for the JV team this year, even though he'd done nothing to improve himself in the off-season. I told him he'd never make the team unless he worked out, and his answer was "Don't friggin' worry. I'll be fine."

The first time I met Frankie was in first grade. He sat next to me, and for some reason, we both started laughing. He might have said something, I might have said something, or maybe it was just a stupid look or something, but we both started laughing—and we couldn't stop. The teacher, Mrs. White, made us both stay after school. The next day, it happened again, and we both received the same punishment. When it happened one more time, we had to go to the principal's office. Mr. Wagner, the principal, seemed to be sort of a nice guy, but we were both scared to death. He talked to us for a while in a stern voice, but then his mood got a little less serious, and he cracked some dopey joke. Well, the joke wasn't too funny, but we both laughed a little to kind of make Mr. Wagner feel good—and it worked. Mr. Wagner laughed right along with us. Then I looked over at Frankie, and we both kind of wondered what the heck we were laughing about, so we started laughing along on our own. Of course, once Frankie and I got to laughing together, there was no way to stop us, so there we were again, laughing our heads off uncontrollably, but ole Mr. Wagner, who must have thought he was Bob Hope or something, was as pleased as punch to think he was such a good comedian.

"Okay. That's enough, boys," Mr. Wagner said. "Let's get back to Mrs. White's class."

Well, we couldn't say anything because we were laughing so uncontrollably, so we just nodded, and Mr. Wagner took us back to Mrs. White's class. By the time we got back to class, we were laughing so hard our stomachs hurt. We waited at the door, and Mr. Wagner advised Mrs. White that he'd had a long talk with us and believed we would behave ourselves. Our stomachs were hurting so much that we finally stopped laughing, but Mr. Wagner tried the same dopey joke on Mrs. White. Well, of course, she didn't think it was funny at all, but we broke out laughing again. That really pleased Mr. Wagner, who apparently had forgotten that the reason we were sent to him in the first place was because we were always laughing. We walked back to our seats and continued laughing throughout the rest of the morning. Mrs. White made us stay after school for the rest of the week.

Eventually, we had to see the school psychologist. The school psychologist was a fat, roly-poly old guy with a red nose named Mr. O'Hirlihy. We were pretty scared when we went to see him. He tried to act nice to make us feel at ease, but he overdid it. Apparently, he didn't know the reason we were sent to him, so he cracked a joke. It was really stupid and even worse than Mr. Wagner's jokes, but it was so bad that it got us laughing again, and we spent most of the interview laughing away with Mr. O'Hirlihy, who was trying to act like Soupy Sales. We had a great time and went back to Mrs. White's class in better spirits than ever. She sentenced us to another week of detention. We later found out that Mr. O'Hirlihy had gotten us mixed up with some other screwed-up kids he was supposed to interview who were suffering from chronic depression. That was why he gave us the Soupy Sales comedy routine. When we went back to him again, we were pretty scared because we figured he was pissed at the mistake he'd made, and we were afraid he might try to pull a Boris Karloff Frankenstein routine instead of a Soupy Sales routine. Well, he was totally serious, and he didn't crack any jokes, but with his red nose and bald head, he didn't much resemble Frankenstein.

We had to see Mr. O'Hirlihy once a week for about a month, until somebody came up with the brilliant idea of making Frankie sit on the side of the room opposite me. That worked pretty well for Mrs. White's class, but Mr. O'Hirlihy was still curious about our laughing fits. One day some lady from New York City came to interview us and said that Columbia University wanted Frankie and me for some child psychology experiment. She said she wanted to study one of our laughing fits and take moving pictures of us and everything. We were excited. We felt like celebrities. My brother even predicted we'd wind up on *The Ed Sullivan Show*. But our mothers wouldn't let us. It was bad enough that the local school system thought we were nuts; our mothers didn't want the whole world to know. The lady psychologist tried to convince our mothers that Frankie and I were special and that perhaps we held the secret to what could make millions of children throughout the world happy. She said it would benefit the world if Frankie and I could be studied. Well, our mothers thought that was a little far-fetched, and Frankie's father said he thought the lady psychologist was a Communist, so they would never sign the release form to allow us to be studied.

Once we were separated in class, our laughing kind of died down, and eventually, everybody forgot about our laughing fits. Every year after that, Frankie and I would always try to sit together at the start of the school year, but after one week and several laughing fits, the teachers would split us up. By the time we got to the fifth grade, they were ready for us, and they would split us up on the first day. Frankie still believed that was why he didn't get into the same section with me in high school. He thought there was a conspiracy to keep us apart. Frankie even got philosophical sometimes when we talked about how they tried to split us up all the time just because we liked to laugh so much. Frankie said the world was basically a pretty sad place, especially for grown-ups, so when grown-ups saw kids having a real good time and laughing away, they got jealous and tried to stop it. I wasn't sure if Frankie was entirely right, but I thought his theory had a lot on the ball. We never could quite figure out why we laughed together so much, but we still had some of that spark left when we got to high school, and I didn't want to lose it.

Good old Frankie was always my best buddy, and regardless of the fact that he'd probably never make the JV team, I wanted him to try. I kind of needed him. He always built up my confidence, and I was going to need it this year. I knew last year's fun and games were over. What a circus that season was. Our only win came against a team with only eight players. Seven were second-stringers, and one was the equipment boy. That happened because the team's bus carrying all the frontline players broke down on the turnpike, and even so, that game was really close. We won 7–5 when Dionne sliced a two-run double into the trees down the right-field line. We did, however, have a few decent excuses for our miserable record freshman year. One was that our two best players were playing JV. Another reason was that our coach was a really nice guy but a terrible coach. He was actually just a history teacher who, for whatever reason, decided to take on the task of coaching the freshman baseball team—a job that most of the big-deal, all-pro gym teachers who thought they were great coaches didn't want to touch. So Mr. Gonzo took on the task.

Mr. Gonzo knew the Civil War inside out, but he didn't seem to know the difference between an inside pitch and an outside pitch. He was the type of coach who didn't believe in stressing the fundamentals. Our pitchers would practice intricate pick-off plays, even though they didn't know how to throw a strike. Our outfielders and infielders would practice elaborate cutoff plays, even though most of us had trouble catching the ball. We'd work on squeeze plays, even though we couldn't bunt, and we'd practice hit-and-run plays, even though we couldn't hit a lick.

Despite the fact that we couldn't hit, throw, or catch, Mr. Gonzo set up an elaborate system of signs to apparently make up for our flaws in the fundamentals. He had signals for everything—take, swing, bunt, squeeze, hit-and-run, steal, pitch-out. Of course, we didn't get to use the signs often because we didn't know how to bunt, hit, or pitch.

One of Mr. Gonzo's favorite signs was the pitch-out. As soon as an opponent's runner got on base, which was often, he'd flash the pitch-out sign to our pitcher and catcher. Sure enough, the runner on first would take off, trying to steal second. Mr. Gonzo felt real proud about always knowing when to expect a steal and call for a pitch-out. The trouble was, our catcher couldn't reach second base. It didn't matter if there was a pitch-out or not; there was no way our catcher was ever going to throw out anybody trying to steal second. I thought the other coaches were well aware of our catcher's throwing deficiency, and I was sure their strategy was simply "If you get on base, run." Anyway, Mr. Gonzo thought he was positively crafty with his pitch-out sign.

Another one of Mr. Gonzo's problems was that he didn't know how to conduct a practice. He was a great believer in delegating authority. He'd delegate the responsibility of hitting fly balls to one of the second-stringers so that the starting outfielders could get some fielding practice. The trouble was, the guy he sent to hit the fly balls could hardly swing the bat, so the outfielders would stand out there for a half hour while the guy would hit weak pop-ups or anemic little grounders. It was nothing like what happened in a real game.

Then Mr. Gonzo would set up batting practice. He wouldn't let our two best pitchers—and calling them the best wasn't saying much—pitch batting practice because he wanted to save their arms for real games, so he was left with an assortment of uncoordinated clunkers who made up the rest of our pitching staff. I don't want to be cruel or anything, but these guys were bad—real bad. They could never throw the ball over the plate, which, of course, didn't help our hitting much since we never saw a strike in batting practice. When batting, we would stand up there, patiently waiting for a good pitch, but soon we'd start getting bored, so we would decide to swing at anything. That would really mess us up because in a game, we'd wind up swinging at everything, including bad pitches. Needless to say, batting practice was a disaster.

After batting practice was mercifully over, old Mr. Gonzo would begin his biggest farce of them all. He would lead us in a drill called game situations, in which he would set up a real-life game situation, and we were supposed to learn what to do in that situation. He'd start with runners on first and second and one out, and a hit-and-run was on. We'd all take the field, and two players would be the base runners. There'd be a batter, but he wouldn't hit the ball. Mr. Gonzo would stand off to the side and hit the ball out of his hand. That way, he could control where the ball was hit. The pitcher would pitch the ball to the catcher, and Mr. Gonzo would hit a ball out to one of us fielders. He'd start with a simple fly ball out to left field, which the left fielder would drop, and the whole situation would be ruined because of course, he was supposed to catch the ball. So Mr. Gonzo would try again—same situation. He then, he hit a grounder to me at short. I caught it, and I had to throw to first because the runners were going, and there was no chance for a double play. Fine. But the first baseman dropped the ball. We tried again. He hit me another grounder. I caught it but threw it two feet over the first baseman's head. We tried again. Mr. Gonzo gave up on me and hit a grounder to the third baseman. Well, the third baseman had moved over to the bag to cover for the steal, so the ball dribbled out into left field. We tried again. He told the third baseman to stay put until the ball was hit, and Mr. Gonzo hit him another grounder. He stayed put. Fine. But the ball went right through his legs. We tried again—same play. He hit another easy grounder to the third baseman. He stayed put. Fine. He caught the ball. Fine. The runners were going, so he had no play except to first. He threw to first. Fine. But he threw the ball two feet over the first baseman's head. We tried again—same situation. This time, Mr. Gonzo figured he might have better luck if he tried the outfield. He hit a fly ball to center field. Well, the center fielder had become bored with all the screwups in the infield, so he wasn't paying attention. He never saw the ball, and it dropped in front of him. We tried again. Mr. Gonzo hit another fly to center. The center fielder was paying attention. Fine. He got under the ball. Fine. But he dropped it. We tried again. Mr. Gonzo hit another fly ball. The fielder caught this one. Great. He saw that the runner from first—who was darn tired from running every time—was slowly going back to first, so he threw the ball to first. Great. But he uncorked a real doozy of a throw that sailed two feet over the first baseman's head. Finally, Mr. Gonzo gave up on that situation and tried another one, but for some reason, he made the situation even harder and more complicated. He must have thought we had the first-and-second, nobody-out hit-and-run situation mastered. This time, he tried a bases-loaded, one-out suicide squeeze. Well, we must have worked on that for about an hour, and we never once got it right. Finally, Mr. Gonzo stopped the futile ordeal when the runner from third base nearly passed out from running home so many times.

In a word, Mr. Gonzo's practices were a disaster. Seriously.

One of Mr. Gonzo's most notable attributes was his patience. He could put up with all kinds of crap and not really get mad. Of course, sometimes he should have gotten mad to get a little respect. But anyway, all in all, he was a patient guy. The only time Mr. Gonzo really blew his stack was at me. It was during the Wayfield game, and of course, we were losing. The score was about 14–3, and I managed to lead off the sixth inning with a solid double down the third-base line. There I was, on second base, and Jonathan, one of our pitchers, was over coaching third. Jonathan and I were good friends, and we kibitzed around a lot, except during a game, because during a game, Jonathan had a way of getting super serious. I mean, we could be losing by eleven runs, and there was Jonathan, talking it up on the third-base coaching lines, shouting encouragement and all kinds of senseless things.

Well, anyway, there I was on second base, kind of pleased with myself for hitting a double, and there was Jonathan with a serious look on his face, flashing signals to me. Now, remember what I said about how Mr. Gonzo had a very professional and intricate system of signs? Well, Jonathan was probably the only person on the team who actually *knew* all the signs, and Jonathan took great pride in his third-base coaching, especially because the third-base coach had the responsibility of relaying the signs from Mr. Gonzo to the batter and the base runners. Well, Jonathan was going through a thousand signs and decoy signs, and all of a sudden, I saw him flash the steal sign. Now, I had pretty good speed, and I ran the bases hard like the Mick did when his legs were still good, but of course, it wasn't easy to steal third, and it was darn stupid to risk it when you were down by eleven runs. So I was stunned. I took a good lead, but when the pitcher pitched, I stayed put. I watched Jonathan again. He went through his stupid sign-giving ritual, and there it was again: the steal sign. The steal sign was a tug on the bill of the cap, followed by two hand claps. With all the decoys Jonathan gave, it could get pretty difficult to pick out the steal sign, but I was positive he gave it, so on the next pitch, I took off for third. *Zap!* They nailed me. It wasn't even close. I brushed off my pants and trotted toward the bench, and old Mr. Gonzo started screaming his head off.

"We're down eleven runs! Why in heaven's name are you trying to steal?"

"Well, Jonathan gave me the steal sign," I said meekly.

"The steal sign?" Mr. Gonzo screamed with smoke coming out of his ears. "What steal sign? I didn't give any signs. We're down eleven runs. Why am I going to give a steal sign?"

I didn't have anything else to say, so I sat down. When the inning ended, I went over to Jonathan and asked him if he had given me the steal sign. Jonathan was as serious as could be.

"Hell no. That wasn't no steal sign. That was just a decoy."

"A decoy?" I said.

"Yeah. They were probably expecting us to try something to get a rally going, so I wanted to try to confuse them by flashing a lot of signs," Jonathan said.

"Confuse *them*?" I said.

"Yeah. Didn't you see that I coughed in between touching the cap and clapping my hands? Coughing is the nullifier sign. It nullifies the previous sign. I kept coughing through the whole darn sequence. What did ya think—I had whooping cough or something? You should have seen that the steal sign was off."

"Yeah, yeah," I said, shaking my head in disgust. But come to think of it, Jonathan was right. As I went out to my position at shortstop, I remembered one boring skull session back in the middle of April when Mr. Gonzo was trying to explain his dopey signs to us. At one point, when most of us were just about asleep—of course, Jonathan was wide awake—Mr. Gonzo told us that a cough nullified any previous sign. Great, huh? Real professional. What a time for Jonathan to use that stupid nullifier sign. That Jonathan was really something.

The first day of JV practice was cold. It was March, and there was still a lot of wet snow around. The fields were wet and muddy in spots and frozen in other spots, so our school had to rely on its vast storehouse of facilities. We used the parking lot. Can you believe it? The stupid high school parking lot—complete with all our favorite teachers' cars. They gave us rubber-coated hardballs to practice with, and I guessed they thought that because the balls were rubber-coated, they wouldn't break anything. Well, Jonathan didn't waste any time in putting that theory to the test. Jonathan and I were warming up together, and it didn't take him long to spot the faded-pink Dodge Dart that belonged to our English teacher. Now, Jonathan was a pretty mischievous fellow. He loved to cause trouble.

He went over to the Dodge Dart and said, "Hey, doesn't this cute little car belong to our lovely English teacher, Miss Stewart?"

"Of course it does, you moron," I said. "Like you didn't know."

"Such an attractive vehicle, isn't it?" Jonathan said.

"Cut the crap," I said.

"Such a practical, functional auto. Just think. Someday I'll be old enough to drive one."

"Cut it out, and let's throw," I said. But Jonathan kept it up.

"Just think. Maybe someday I'll have a car like this."

"Cut the crap," I said, and we finally started throwing. But Jonathan stayed right by the car, with his back to the driver's side.

"Hey, Jonathan, why don't you move away from that stupid car? What if one of my throws is a little wild?"

"Gee, wouldn't that be a shame? It might hit Miss Stewart's lovely little auto."

"Cut it out, Jonathan," I said, clenching my teeth in annoyance.

"But gee, don't worry. I'll protect this fine mechanical specimen. And anyway, these balls are only rubber," Jonathan said.

Just then, as I was throwing one back to Jonathan, he said, "Okay, have it your way," and he abruptly turned and walked away as my throw sailed right at Miss Stewart's car.

*Bam!* The ball slammed right into the car door and made the loudest noise imaginable, which echoed off the walls of the school and reverberated throughout the whole stupid parking lot. Everybody stopped what he was doing and looked at me. I put my hands on my head and tried to cover my face with my glove. One of the coaches yelled, "Hey, buddy, will you move away from the cars or learn how to throw a ball like a ballplayer?" Some of the other guys laughed, and I was so darned embarrassed I wanted to just crawl under Miss Stewart's car. Of course, the one who was laughing the most was Jonathan.

"You moron!" I yelled.

Jonathan regained his composure enough to say with complete seriousness, "Nice throw."

"You moron!" I yelled again, and I could feel my face turning red. Then Jonathan went over to the car to inspect the damage.

"Hey, look," he said. "Nothing is broken. I guess that's why they make us use these here rubber-coated hardballs."

As much as I was dedicated to baseball and as much as I liked playing it, I had to admit it wasn't meant to be played in cold weather. After we warmed up for a while on that first day of practice—or tried to warm up—the coaches had us take a few laps around the parking lot.

What fun. Then, of course, they put us through the rituals of calisthenics, which everybody hated and cheated on anyway. We started with jumping jacks. I always noticed that high school ballplayers tried to maintain their cool while performing their various athletic tasks, whether shooting a layup, catching a fly ball, throwing a football, or whatever else. Maintaining your cool was just about as important as doing whatever you were doing. However, it got pretty tough to maintain your cool when doing jumping jacks because there was no way to do a jumping jack without looking like a complete fool. Coaches probably felt that jumping jacks instilled a little humility in their cool-conscious troops. It was funny to watch the different styles of the guys doing their jumping jacks. Most guys cheated on the extension of their arms, not because they were too tired and out of shape or because they were too lazy to do the exercise correctly but because they didn't want to look so darn silly.

"All right, you bunch of goof-offs. Let me demonstrate the correct way to do a jumping jack," the coach would say. Then he would do a few perfect jumping jacks. He would stretch his legs out real far and bounce up and down, spreading his arms out really wide. He looked like a fool, and of course, he knew it too, but he also knew he would only have to do two or three jumping jacks as a demonstration. He knew we'd have to spend a half hour doing them and would look like fools every minute. Coaches loved to see their players look like fools during practice. Seriously. There couldn't be any other reason they'd put us through some of that crap.

After jumping jacks, we did sit-ups—on the freezing asphalt. Wonderful. Then we did various stretching exercises, which the coaches told us we should naturally want to do on our own. Then we did a few push-ups, and finally, we split up according to positions. There would be three groups: infielders, outfielders, and pitchers and catchers. Of course, by that time, the sun was down fairly low, and it was getting even colder. They threw out a few bases and set up an infield. Since the varsity and the JV were together, there were five or six of us at each position, and one coach was hitting us grounders. You can do the math. There were four positions—1B, 2B, SS, 3B—with six guys at each position. That meant each player would get every twenty-fourth grounder, and he'd better make the most of it because it would be twenty-three more grounders before he got the next one. Plus, of course, everybody wanted to look good on the first day. First impressions were important. Well, I was second to last in the shortstop line, and I handled my first grounder—the seventeenth grounder of the season—well, except I threw it wildly to first, and the ball wound up rolling around under some of the faculty cars. Fortunately, it didn't go near Miss Stewart's car, but unfortunately, I was quickly gaining a reputation for a somewhat erratic arm. They even started to call me the Wrecker, a nickname I never grew to appreciate.

Frankie was over at second base, and as expected, he was having problems. He told me he was going out for second base this year because his arm was too weak for the outfield, but of course, I had to point out that the reason they always stuck him in the outfield—always right field—was because that was where the opposition was least likely to hit the ball. Anyway, Frankie always had his reasons, and he was always too thickheaded to change. With each grounder, it got colder and colder, and of course, our coach kept trying to hit the ball harder and harder. The ball started to sting when I caught it. The ball would sting so much that I kind of envied Frankie, who let practically every ball go right through his legs. After we had our chance with a grounder, we'd run to the back of the line to wait and freeze. We'd start doing modified jumping jacks with no concern for style just to keep from freezing. Some of us speculated that we might be the first team in baseball history to forfeit our first five games due to frostbite.

The next day was pretty much the same. I threw with Frankie, who never stopped complaining about how his whole body hurt from the first workout. I told Frankie he was sore because of his off-season habits. Frankie tried to assure me that he was in tip-top shape, and he was sore because of the cold weather and the coaches working him too hard. I had to agree with him about that.

Throwing the ball back and forth was another kind of baseball ritual, and the coaches would have us do it before practice to warm up. When we were kids, our mothers would say, "Why don't you boys go out and play catch?" They did this to prevent us from wrecking the house when we got too restless. Now we were supposed big-shot high school ball players, and when the coaches would start warm-ups before practice, they'd put out a bag of balls.

We'd grab one, pair up, and "throw," as we called it. We would never "play catch"—even though that was what we were doing. After all, we were trying to be big-shot high school ball players and wouldn't be caught dead playing catch. It was much cooler to throw.

Actually, throwing wasn't too bad. It was a good way to goof off with your buddies and shoot the breeze. Jonathan was the king of goofing off, and Frankie was the prince of shooting the breeze. Frankie was never at a loss for words. He could go one on one yap-trapping with anybody. Most of the time, he would be complaining about something, and the rest of the time, either he would be laughing, or somebody would be laughing at him. Frankie could take a joke reasonably well, and the older guys constantly harassed him about his lack of athletic ability. The coaches also liked to pick on Frankie. It was all good-natured, and the kidding always kept everybody loose, especially me. I really needed Frankie around. After all, he was my best friend. We always walked home together, and he was an encouragement to me. Since my biggest problem, aside from a lack of any high-quality athletic ability, was my confidence, I relied on him. I was worried about whether Frankie would make the team, and since this year was gonna be different, I was worried that I might lose Frankie and have to make it on my own. Of course, I couldn't let on to anybody how I felt, but I sure was worried. I kept trying to encourage Frankie to get his act together, but it was hard. Frankie was one of those people with absolutely no willpower. He'd do almost anything anybody told him to do—especially if it would somehow get him into trouble. Of course, he'd listen to anybody but me.

I knew Frankie and I were drifting apart when Frankie decided he didn't want to watch *Star Trek* anymore. It might not seem like a big deal, but we were both really big *Star Trek* fans, and I couldn't understand why Frankie would give up our favorite show. Frankie had been going over to Murray's house on Saturday nights since last fall, and I had already conceded that loss, but our Friday nights with the old crew of the *Enterprise* had become pretty much a sacred routine. We'd watch the show and then play some Ping-Pong in Frankie's basement, and then we'd sneak out for a hamburger and hang out for a while. Frankie had Spock down really well, but his best imitation was of Scottie. He would do that Scottish accent for hours. He'd order his burgers with that dopey accent, and then I'd try to convince the cute counter girl that Frankie was my long-lost cousin on holiday from the British Isles. Then of course we would start laughing and nobody would fall for our act, but it was fun to try.

*Star Trek* was kind of my outlet to a dream world. I'd always liked science fiction, and to me, *Star Trek* was sci-fi at its best. When the show first came on a few years ago, it was all the rage, and Frankie and I really took to it. I liked to dream about the stars and what lay in those deep black spaces out in the nighttime sky. When I went home from Frankie's on those frigid winter nights, when the sky was packed with stars twinkling away like mad, I would stand out in the cold as long as I could and just gaze up at the stars and pick out the constellations. Orion had always been my favorite—kind of a buddy to me. He was by far the easiest constellation to pick out, and throughout the winter, he stood up there, dominating the sky. On my way home from Frankie's, I always cut through a small field. It was fairly dark, but there were enough streetlights in the distance so that it wasn't too scary. I liked to stop there in the winter to gaze at the stars and at old Orion. I'd stand there until I just about froze. It was just so peaceful and serene, and with the smooth *Star Trek* theme song flowing through my mind, I felt content. Then I'd realize how cold I was, and I'd tear off through the snow and down the street to my house. In a flash, I'd be upstairs in bed, snuggled tightly—safe and secure under three blankets.

Well, last winter, I could see that things were gonna be different. Frankie didn't have much interest in *Star Trek*. Everybody seemed to care only about *Laugh-In* and the Smothers Brothers and, of course, going over to the parties at Murray's house to get drunk. Frankie was no different. One Friday night last February, I went over to Frankie's house to watch *Star Trek*, but Frankie's mother said Frankie was out. She said he was at the library, working on a term paper, but I knew different. She invited me to stay until Frankie got back, but I knew he'd be out late at Murray's house. I stayed for a while anyway and watched *Star Trek* as Spock outsmarted some alien without even the trace of a smile, and the show ended with Captain Kirk and Bones making some crack about how Spock never laughed at anything. They started laughing hysterically, but all they could get out of old Spock was a partially raised eyebrow. I said good night and headed home. I made a quick stop in the field and looked up at old Orion, but he was kind of slipping down toward the western horizon. He looked as if he were falling. I knew that was a sign of the changing season. Springtime was coming, and I was losing a friend.

Things really started to change between me and Frankie when we entered the ninth grade. It was the first time all of us kids from Sherman Elementary School got split up. They split us up according to who was smarter, which actually meant who got better grades. Of course, Frankie never had cared much about getting good grades, so he and I got split up. Frankie wasn't any dumber than I was, but he messed around a little more than I did. Frankie never took things seriously in grammar school. He always did well in subjects he liked, such as science, but he couldn't stand math and English, so he always did lousy in those subjects. When we went to high school, they stuck poor Frankie in one of the rowdier sections. When a person was put into a rowdy group like that and was a follower like Frankie was, he or she was headed for trouble. My only real influence now over Frankie was with baseball, and that was quickly slipping away. I could see it happening, but I couldn't do anything about it.

By the third day of practice, it was evident that Frankie's chances of making the JV baseball team were slim. Frankie was setting the record for most misplayed grounders. I tried to talk to Frankie about it when we walked home from practice, but he wouldn't listen. He kept saying that he was getting all the bad hops and that it was impossible to catch a stupid rubber-coated hardball off a stupid asphalt parking lot anyway. I tried to point out to him that most of us were able to catch grounders off the asphalt parking lot, but Frankie still wouldn't listen. He said to just wait until we got out onto the field. I wanted to tell him that he might get cut by the time we switched over to the field, but I didn't have the heart—and I didn't want to believe it myself.

I offered to hit him some grounders that Sunday afternoon, and Frankie said, "Sure," but when I went over to his house, he was still in his pajamas and said he couldn't play. He said he'd been at a great party at Murray's and had started out drinking burgundy wine but switched over to Boone's Farm apple wine. He said he loved the Boone's Farm and had drunk the whole bottle. He said he'd had a great time last night, but his stomach wasn't too great today. Then he told me to make sure I didn't tell his mother, because she'd kill him if she knew he was drinking. We watched a little of the basketball game on TV, but then Frankie started moaning and said he had a terrible headache and wanted to go lie down. So I walked home. It was sunny but still cold and windy. There were still lumps of snow around, mostly by the street and the driveways, where it had been piled real high after the snowstorms. The snow piles were glistening in the sun, but it was still cold, and it didn't seem like spring was only two weeks away. Somehow, I wasn't looking forward to baseball season. I knew I was going to have to face it without Frankie. It was going to be different, and it didn't seem like it was going to be any fun.

Frankie didn't make it to school on Monday or Tuesday, and consequently, he missed practice both days. When he showed up on Wednesday, he was his old jovial self, kibitzing around with everyone and telling his stories about Saturday night. A few other guys had been at the party too, so we were all treated to several different accounts of the same party while we were throwing. Everyone agreed that Frankie had drunk a whole bottle of Boone's Farm and that it had been a great party. There were, however, different stories as to where Frankie had spent most of the night after he had drunk the infamous bottle of Boone's Farm. One guy said Frankie had spent considerable time in a newly invented yoga position over the toilet bowl as he threw up for three straight hours in exactly fifteen-minute intervals. One version had Frankie spending the whole night passed out on the porch, saved from freezing only by the high alcohol content of his blood. Everybody thought it was hilarious, but it made me a little sick to my stomach.

By Wednesday of the second week of practice, Frankie's performance still had not improved. As Frankie and I walked home, we reminisced about old Mrs. White's class and all the trouble we'd caused. We then started laughing hysterically, and we laughed all the way home. The next day, we found out that Frankie had been cut from the team.

# CHAPTER 4

# Jonathan

With Frankie gone, I relied more and more on Jonathan.
I'd only known Jonathan since freshman year, and he
was a trip and a half. He was the first Negro kid I'd ever
gotten to know, and we'd become good friends. Now
one very important thing I learned as soon as I got to
know Jonathan was that he hated the terms Negro and
especially colored. He made it clear to me that the proper
term was black. He said *black is beautiful* and that I better
get with it or I'd be considered an ignorant honky. I didn't
think honky was a very nice term either but sometimes it
wasn't worth arguing with Jonathan. No black kids went
to my grammar school, so I never got to meet any until
high school. My town had five grammar schools: three of
them had nothing but white kids; one, Roosevelt School,
had nothing but black kids; and Chestnut School, where
Jonathan went, had a mixture. The kids in my town were
a little worried when we were ready to go to high school
because there would be a lot of black kids there and we
didn't know what to expect. It was rumored that some

of the kids in my neighborhood actually went to the all-white Catholic school just to avoid going to school with black kids. Some of us were a little scared, what with some of the goings-on at Roosevelt School. There were stories of robberies and some fights in that section of town. Of course, everybody was just generally uncertain of black people anyway, so it was quite an experience when we all made it to high school, and there were all these black kids.

Well, Jonathan was nothing to be scared of, even though he for darn sure knew there were a lot of white kids scared of him, and boy, he knew how to get the most out of that fear. Jonathan was as black as a person could get, and he could put on the meanest scowl when he wanted to. But he could also act like a moron just like any white kid, and he was basically harmless and likeable, as were most of his friends, who I eventually got to know. Of course, I couldn't say the same about some of the kids from Roosevelt School. Some of those kids were as mean as could be, and they weren't acting. Roosevelt School was situated over in a corner of town where only black people lived. I had never been there and probably never would have dared to go there, except that Roosevelt Field was the JV field, and I would be spending a lot of time there with the JV team.

Many of the kids who came out of Roosevelt Elementary School seemed to have had lots of problems, and some didn't last long in high school, but a lot of them were really good athletes. I got to know one guy, Ricky, in my homeroom. Ricky was a pretty good guy, but he could never get his mind on his schoolwork. He told me his father worked two jobs but his parents were always fighting over money, which they didn't have much of in the first place. He was always getting into fights and then getting suspended. He had a reputation for being a good fighter, but when one got to know the guy, he was all right. I could never figure out why he got into so many fights. Eventually, he just kind of faded out of my homeroom class, and that was it. I heard later on from Jonathan that Ricky had dropped out. I asked why, and Jonathan sarcastically said, "To pursue a career in street crime." Well, street crime was not what Jonathan was interested in. He once confided in me that he wanted to be the first black president of the United States. If anybody, black or white, could become president, it was Jonathan.

Jonathan was really smart, but he was also a real character. Like I said, he knew the white kids were generally pretty scared of him, and he knew how to play that up. He was smart enough to take on the teachers with his brains and clever enough to take on the tough kids with his blackness. Jonathan was in a lot of my classes because we were in the advanced class. There were only two other black kids in the advanced class, and they were both very quiet, so Jonathan stuck out. He could outsmart most of the teachers pretty well. They all thought he was serious and a hard worker, but behind their backs, he was the biggest kibitzer in the whole class. He always tried to sit in the back of the classroom, which was rather easy because his last name began with a *Y*, and when a seating arrangement was made alphabetically, he was always the last one. Even in the classes where seating wasn't done alphabetically, he would go straight for the last seat in the last row. Once, a teacher who didn't believe in the alphabetical system asked Jonathan why he insisted on sitting in the back. Jonathan said that as a black person, he was used to sitting in the back behind white people. Jonathan always liked to refer to himself as black. He hated being called colored or Negro. Anyway, all his fellow classmates sure enough knew why Jonathan sat in the last seat in the last row: so he could crack jokes with less chance of getting caught.

Jonathan had our English teacher bamboozled. She was old and grouchy, and nobody really liked her except the brownnosers. Well, Jonathan had a different technique for his brownnosing. He called it blacknosing. Old Miss Stewart didn't really know how to handle adolescents. Somehow, she always managed to get the advanced English classes, such as ours, so she had it a little easier than teachers in some of the other classes, who mostly practiced crowd control. Miss Stewart was lucky because she escaped the rigors of crowd control by getting to teach so-called good students. The good students consisted of about ten kids who were genuinely smart, about fifteen of us who were smart enough to know how to get good marks on the stupid tests, a handful of brownnosers, and one blacknoser: Jonathan. Now, Jonathan wasn't dumb. He was real smart. However, he admitted that he rarely had to use his intelligence because he said it was easier to use his blacknosing technique, which he had down to a science in Miss Stewart's advanced English class. The basics of blacknosing came from the fact that most teachers, especially Miss Stewart, really didn't know how to handle an intelligent black kid. They seemed more patient with a black kid who was trying than with a white kid because they thought all black kids weren't as smart as white kids. Miss Stewart was a prime example. She'd been teaching the advanced English class for a long time and had had few black kids, so Jonathan knew how to handle Miss Stewart perfectly with his blacknosing technique. He would say, "Yes, Miss Stewart," and "Oh, I didn't know that, Miss Stewart," whenever he spoke. Jonathan said his secret was to never act too smart, or else he'd really blow her mind. He knew that all he had to do was act like he was trying, and Miss Stewart would be so impressed that he'd get good marks for sure. That way, Jonathan didn't have to study too much for exams because he knew that even if he got lousy marks on a few tests, when the marking period came around, that old E for effort would turn into an A for A1 blacknosing.

Miss Stewart was the usual kind of dumb teacher who would always ask the class if we had any questions after she explained some boring stuff about how to diagram sentences or footnote some stupid term paper. Of course, everybody either wasn't listening to her or was too bored with the whole subject to want to ask a question about it, even the brownnosers—but not our superstar blacknoser. He'd come up with some ridiculous, insignificant question that would start Miss Stewart off on some dumb, detailed explanation more boring than the first explanation. Jonathan would sit there nodding in fascination. Of course, Miss Stewart felt great upon seeing that when she spewed out all that boring information, someone was actually interested—which, of course, was untrue because Jonathan couldn't have cared less. Jonathan had his system so well refined that he never asked a question that was too hard for Miss Stewart to answer, because he knew she got annoyed when someone showed everybody how limited her knowledge was by asking a difficult question. Some of the smart kids always fell into that trap. They got really involved in a subject and then started asking all kinds of questions, which, according to Jonathan, actually showed how dumb they were, because if they were really smart like he was, they would know the limits of Miss Stewart's knowledge. Jonathan sure knew Miss Stewart's limits. She thought he was a sweet boy. Little did she know that on Jonathan's way to becoming the first black president, he had become the first black Eddie Haskell—like in the old *Leave It to Beaver* show.

But Jonathan couldn't resist the temptation to occasionally blow Miss Stewart's mind. Of course, even though she thought he was sweet, she still would not have liked to run into Jonathan alone on a dark street, so a few times, Jonathan had to get his kicks. One time, he did an unbelievable book report on a book called *Native Son* by a black author. Jonathan described in great detail a part of the book in which a young black guy kills a white girl and then chops her up into little pieces and throws her into a potbellied stove. It sounded like a positively wild book, and we could see that Miss Stewart was really cringing. But Jonathan read the report in the sweetest blacknoser voice we'd ever heard, and poor Miss Stewart didn't know what to do. This big black guy, who she wanted to believe was sweet and a hard worker but who terrified her deep down, was standing in front of the class, talking as sweetly as could be in disgusting detail about some black guy chopping up some white girl and burning up the pieces in a potbellied stove. When we got out of that class that day, Jonathan and I didn't stop laughing for two hours. Oh, and I really had to read that book!

We were also in the advanced social studies class together, and it was actually a really good class, which was unusual. We had a good teacher too, Mr. Fisher, which was also pretty unusual. Jonathan excelled in social studies, and he did it with a minimal amount of blacknosing. He got into a lot of arguments with Mr. Fisher about the war in Vietnam. Mr. Fisher went into a detailed explanation about something called the domino theory, which was supposed to explain why the United States was sending troops over to fight in Vietnam. Jonathan said he had developed his own theory called the Parcheesi theory, which said that if all the politicians who wanted to send troops to Vietnam would just sit down and play a simple game of Parcheesi, then nobody would get hurt. Jonathan said he had decided that dominoes were far too dangerous.

Jonathan was also into politics. He told me last winter that President Johnson was going to have a pretty hard time getting reelected if he kept the war going. Jonathan said that now would be a good time for a black man to run for president, but he was a little too young to run. He said that Dr. Martin Luther King Jr. would be a good candidate except that all the honky white folks would never vote for him because he was black. We had a mock presidential election last fall to preview the upcoming real-life 1968 presidential election. We had Democratic and Republican primaries. There wasn't much interest in our Republican primary, and Rockefeller got our nomination. However, in the Democratic primary, there was a lot of debate, with Jonathan supporting Martin Luther King Jr. and mean-mouthing President Johnson. Mr. Fisher tried to explain to Jonathan that in real life, Martin Luther King Jr. would have no chance of getting the nomination, because he didn't even participate in party politics, but Jonathan wouldn't hear of it. He said that the classroom exercise wasn't real life and that the rules of the game were that we could nominate whoever we wanted—except, of course, Mr. Fisher wouldn't allow the nomination of crazy comedian Tommy Smothers. Jonathan was pretty sly in accusing Mr. Fisher of being prejudiced for questioning Martin Luther King Jr.'s credentials. We had speeches and assigned delegates and went through the whole bit. We even had one kid act like Walter Cronkite, and he gave a news report on the proceedings. Jonathan wanted to get some balloons, but Mr. Fisher said no way. When we finally took the vote, the results were extremely close, with Bobby Kennedy just beating out Johnson. Martin Luther King Jr. got only two votes. King's two votes seemed strange because there were three black kids in the class, and everybody had expected them to vote as a block for Dr. King. I expected Jonathan to put up a stink over the missing vote, but he didn't make much of it and seemed content with the way the vote had turned out. Later on, I got him to confide in me about why he wasn't concerned about the vote.

"Oh, I know who didn't vote for Brother Martin. It was me," Jonathan said with a huge grin.

"What?" I said.

"Yeah, of course. I knew the Doc wouldn't win, so I voted for Bobby. Out of all the whites, Bobby's the only one who cares a hoot about us black folks. Sure, LBJ seemed like he did until he started messing around with that war of his. As for Dr. King, I just wanted to scare you white folks into thinking that if we blacks voted together, we'd cause you a heck of a lot of trouble. So then you guys decided to vote for the only one of your candidates who could appease us black folks without us getting one of our own in office, so we wouldn't go around rioting. So I figured I'd jump on board and give old Bobby a little push. And it worked. That's politics, my friend."

I wasn't quite sure what he meant, but I thought everybody had voted for Bobby Kennedy just because he was the best looking. Bobby easily beat Rockefeller in our general election.

Jonathan was not exactly our best baseball player, but he managed to get the job done most of the time. There wasn't much chance he'd be a starting pitcher for JV, but I thought the coaches kept him more because he looked mean than anything else. The coaches either thought Jonathan looked so mean that opposing batters would be afraid to hit against him or were too afraid to cut him. Jonathan didn't have to put on any nice, intelligent black kid act to play sports. The coaches weren't much interested in intelligence to begin with since most coaches weren't too intelligent, and they certainly didn't want a bunch of high school kids to outsmart them. So Jonathan was content to just act mean. He said that as a black person, it was his true nature to act mean in the unjust white-dominated society. He said, "That's the real reason why black kids do so good in sports. It's not because they're dumb or because they've been educationally and culturally deprived. And it's not because they are better natural athletes, having spent so much time running away from wild animals in the jungles of Africa, running away from wild slave owners in the South, or running away from wild cops in the cities. Blacks are good in sports because it is the easiest socially acceptable way to be mean." According to Jonathan, since being mean was natural for blacks in the unjust white-dominated society, it was natural for them to excel in sports. Well, Jonathan didn't exactly excel in sports, but he sure did excel in meanness when he wanted to.

Jonathan didn't talk much during practice, and he was usually serious—except when he was pulling one of his practical jokes. He didn't even talk much to the other black kids. They were a little suspicious about Jonathan, not because he was mean but because he was so different. Jonathan could jive around a lot if he wanted to, but they also knew he hung around with a lot of white kids and was in all the smart classes. But Jonathan was careful not to be condescending to the other black players. Although he was worlds apart in many ways, he did know the basic behavior, and that was to act mean. Jonathan was a real champ at that. He told me he would practice his scowl in the mirror for hours, and anyone who ever caught a glimpse of Jonathan's scowl would have to believe him.

Jonathan's favorite baseball player was Bob Gibson. Jonathan said he liked a lot of the black stars, such as Willie Mays, Hank Aaron, and Elston Howard, but he liked Bob Gibson the most because Gibson was the meanest. Anyone who ever watched Gibson pitch would see that Jonathan was right. Now that Sandy Koufax had retired, Gibson probably had the best fastball in the major leagues, except Gibson didn't seem to have quite as much control as Koufax had. Gibson had a reputation for hitting batters. Some people thought it was because Gibson just didn't have good control. Jonathan said Gibson had great control and hit so many batters because he tried to hit them. Jonathan said Gibson tried to hit batters because he was mean. Jonathan really admired that. Jonathan had the same reputation for hitting batters in our league, and everybody knew he could be pretty mean, but we also knew that Jonathan hit so many batters because he had lousy control. Jonathan had a real good fastball. A lot of times, he threw his fastball way inside, and he proudly called it his Bob Gibson brush-back pitch; however, he also threw his fastball way outside, into the dirt, and over the catcher's head sometimes. Jonathan didn't have any names for those pitches.

Jonathan's family was reasonably normal, except maybe for his dopey kid sister, Lendora, who was eleven years old and a real pain. Jonathan once confided that he could handle almost anybody and could even have handled Adolph Hitler if he'd had to, but sometimes he just couldn't handle Lendora. Last year when Jonathan ran an unsuccessful campaign for class president he got nonstop criticism from Lendora. She kept saying that Jonathan didn't know how to successfully connect with his voters.

"She's a real dang know-it-all," Jonathan complained. "But I have to admit she warned me about having my father help me write my stump speech. He had me going on and on about having a dream that tenth graders and ninth graders could get along. Lendora said the speech was too idealistic and boring. She said I should have just promised everybody a wild Christmas party. After losing the election, I hate to admit it, but I think that little pipsqueak was right."

Actually, despite her nagging, I thought Lendora was a big fan of her brother. She came to several of our freshman baseball games, and a person had to be quite a fan to come to one of those games, especially if he or she was rooting for Jonathan. But we could always hear her in the bleachers, though of course, she didn't do much cheering, because there wasn't much to cheer about the way we played. She especially liked to pick on old Mr. Gonzo, which was all right with us players. We all thought Mr. Gonzo could use a little criticism. She was also great at booing the umpire. No matter what an umpire called, if the call was against our team, Lendora would boo him. One time, an umpire actually stopped the game, came over to the bleachers, and asked Lendora to keep quiet. She looked pretty darn scared when he came over to her, and she shut up real fast—but not for long. About an inning later, she started all over again.

One time, she almost caused a real rhubarb when Jonathan was pitching. Jonathan started out pitching okay but soon began having his usual control problems. Of course, Lendora kept cheering him on. At one point, she really started to get on this one batter, calling him a chump and a puppy dog. Then she yelled for Jonathan to throw one under his chin, and sure enough, Jonathan chose that time to throw one of his patented Bob Gibson brush-back pitches, which was so inside that the batter had no chance whatsoever to get out of the way, and the ball hit him right in the back. Well, the batter didn't take too kindly to being hit in the back, and he was already pissed because of Lendora's razzing, so on his way to first base, he started yelling at Jonathan and coming at him. Jonathan didn't say anything. He didn't even move, and actually, it looked like he was pretty scared. Then, all of a sudden, some of the guys from the other team got off the bench and started to head out toward Jonathan, so then our guys started coming from their positions. It looked like Jonathan was scared and in need of some help, and it also looked like we were headed for a genuine rhubarb, but then I saw that old Jonathan, just as the guy was getting right up next to him, put on one of his all-time meanest, nastiest scowls. The batter put on the brakes super fast. At the same time, some of the other guys on our team who were black put on their meanest oppressed-black-person scowls, and the other team, which all white kids, slowed down a bit. Well, by that time, the stupid umpires and coaches had jumped up and were trying to calm things down. They tried to act all professional and kept saying, "Calm down, gentlemen"—as if calling this wild bunch of adolescents gentlemen would somehow make us act like gentlemen. The other team's coach actually tried to restrain the batter from going at Jonathan, but everybody could see that it was just an act because the batter was too scared to go at Jonathan with Jonathan looking so mean and he was probably pretty darn happy his coach was there to help with his little act. There was a little more yelling and stuff, but things quieted down soon enough. Jonathan went on to pitch a pretty lousy inning. The other team scored three runs, with Jonathan providing three more walks but, fortunately, no more hit batters. However, we had won a moral victory, which we liked to consider more important than winning a game, since we were always more likely to win a moral victory than a ball game. When we got back to the bench, of course Lendora had to add her two cents.

"Next time, hit 'im in the head," she said.

# CHAPTER 5

# Peanuts, Cracker Jack, and Peep Shows

The first time I ever went to a ball game without my father or brother was last year with Jonathan. Unfortunately, it was to a Mets game. Somehow, Jonathan's father could always get ahold of great tickets, but they were always to a dopey Mets game. Jonathan didn't care about the Mets either, but that time Jonathan got lucky and the Mets were playing the Cardinals, and Bob Gibson was scheduled to pitch. It was tough to convince my mother that I'd be all right going to New York without an adult, but my good old dad took my side, and I got permission to go. Of course, I thought my dad took my side because he figured it was about time he got out of the chore of taking the kids to a stupid baseball game every year, but I kind of felt sorry for my dad. I might have hurt his feelings a little, because even though he wouldn't have admitted it,

I thought he really did like taking us to ball games. It was sort of his fatherly responsibility to take the kids to the ball game, but now it was as if I didn't need him anymore. But heck, how long did a kid have to be escorted around by his parents? I was glad he stuck up for me no matter the reason, and I decided that when I got older and was on my own and had my own car and everything, I'd always ask my dad first if he wanted to come to a ball game with me. Of course, it wouldn't be a dopey Mets game.

When I finally got permission to go, I still had one rather large hurdle to get over: my mother wanted to meet this "Jonathan boy," as she said. Well, we were going to catch the New York bus by my house to head out to the old ballpark, so I told my mom Jonathan would stop in on the way. I had told my parents about Jonathan a few times before, but I didn't think I'd ever mentioned the fact that Jonathan was black. Somehow, I kind of thought that if they'd known Jonathan was black, they might have thought of some excuse why I couldn't go to the game—even my father. They probably would have said we had to go over to my grandfather's house or I had to cut the grass, rake the leaves, vacuum the pool, or clean the garage—all on an emergency basis. Fortunately, I never told them Jonathan was black.

When Jonathan came over that Saturday afternoon, it must have been the first time a black person other than the garbage man ever walked through our neighborhood. I knew for a fact that when Jonathan came through our front door, it was the first time a black person had stepped foot in our house. I had to give my mother credit: she didn't faint or even get upset at all. However, I thought somebody in the neighborhood had called the cops because a police car drove by the house a few minutes after Jonathan walked in. My parents were pretty darn cordial, and of course, Jonathan did his best nice-little-black-kid routine, so he seemed to hit it off rather well with my parents. Jonathan carefully explained that his father got tickets occasionally from a friend who worked for some big company, and Jonathan had gone many times with his father and a few times with his other friends. He explained that he knew exactly how to get to Shea Stadium, which was so easy that even my mother remembered from going to the World's Fair a few years ago.

Jonathan explained that he really wasn't much of a Mets fan to my father, who was pretty glad to hear that. He said he was a St. Louis Cardinals fan, and his favorite players were Curt Flood, Bob Gibson, and—get this—Roger Maris. Good old former Yankee star Roger Maris, the other half of the M&M boys—that was just what my father wanted to hear. My father then went into his favorite story about taking us to the game in which ole Rog hit his world-famous sixty-first home run. My father liked to go into great detail about that game whenever he got a chance because it had been such a historic occasion. Of course, he liked to make everybody think he planned it that way, when in actuality, my brother and I had been bugging him to take us to our yearly baseball game all summer that year, and he always had some kind of excuse about why we couldn't go. Well, old Roger hit his sixty-first to beat Babe Ruth's record in the last game of the regular season—which was also the last chance my father had to take us to a ball game in 1961, since there was no chance he'd come up with tickets to the World Series. So in actuality, my father *had* to take us to that game, and ole Rog just happened to hit his sixty-first on that day. But my father liked to tell the story as if he were as much of a hero as Maris. Well, it was a good story the way my father told it anyway.

But since when was my good buddy Jonathan, the ultimate Bob Gibson fan, a Roger Maris fan? I asked him later, and he told me he'd remembered that I had gone to that historic game, and he'd guessed that my father would probably like to brag about going to the game. Jonathan had figured that would be a great way to get in good with my father. At first, I thought it was just another example of Jonathan's conniving schemes to get his way, but then I figured that since it made my father happy to tell his old story about Roger Maris's sixty-first home run, it was a nice gesture. But I knew I still had to watch that Jonathan.

The game was no big deal. Gibson mowed down the lowly Mets with ease. By the ninth inning, the Mets had managed only two hits, and Gibson had a comfortable 2–0 lead. Jonathan was a little disappointed because Gibson hadn't hit any batters, but surprisingly, Jonathan was ready to go. It seemed as if Jonathan was always one step ahead of everybody and always had to get a jump on things. However, I was a bit puzzled as to why Jonathan was in such a rush to leave, when his idol was pitching such a gem of a game. Of course, Jonathan hadn't let me in on his plans for our after-ball-game activities.

As the ninth inning started, we headed out. We rushed down the fancy Shea Stadium escalators and past all the souvenir vendors, who were selling a lot of Mets junk. They were also selling some Cardinals banners and some Bob Gibson buttons, but none of that interested Jonathan, who was headed as fast as he could out to the trains, in a big rush to get home. To do what, I had no idea. We ran up the stairs to the trains, and there was one waiting. Just as we hopped on, we heard a roar from the crowd way out there in the distance.

"Gibby probably struck out the side," Jonathan said.

"Then why the heck would the stupid Mets fans cheer?" I said.

"Respect," Jonathan said as the train took off.

We whizzed past the jumble of buildings and narrow streets, and I saw some of the leftover stuff from the World's Fair. I was a bit disappointed that we left so early. My brother and I always made it a point to beg our father to let us stay until the last out, no matter what, when we went with him. He'd always act pretty pissed off and say we'd get into tons of traffic if we stayed till the end. But we were stubborn. Then we'd always stop for some dopey souvenirs. But we never left before the last out. Now there I was, out on my own without any parents telling me what to do, and Jonathan was tearing around as if he'd never get to leave the house if he didn't get back home on time. At first, I thought maybe Jonathan was trying to make sure he got me home early so my parents would know they could trust him despite the fact that he was black. But I couldn't believe that—not Jonathan. He could have handled my parents easily enough even if we'd come home at twelve midnight. I was sure he'd have an excuse.

I asked him again, "What's the hurry?"

"I want to beat the crowd," Jonathan said.

"Jeez, Jonathan. There was only fifteen thousand," I said.

"Yeah, but I don't want to miss the bus home," Jonathan said.

"There's plenty of buses," I said.

When we got to the Port Authority Bus Terminal, we hurried off the train and on through the tunnels. Then, all of a sudden, Jonathan stopped short and decided he wanted a hot dog. So we went over to a slimy underground hot dog stand, and Jonathan bought himself a hot dog.

"I thought you were in a big hurry," I said.

"I am, but I'm starved," Jonathan said.

"What time does the bus leave?" I asked.

"Ah, let me see." Jonathan took a big bite out of his stupid hot dog and then pulled the bus schedule out of his pocket. "What time is it?" he asked.

"It's four thirty," I said.

"Dang. Are you sure?" Jonathan asked.

"Yeah," I said.

"Well, the bus leaves in three minutes."

"Well, let's get going," I said.

"Hey! Lemme finish my hot dog, will ya?" Jonathan said. He acted like he was mad. "We ain't never gonna make it up to that bus anyway."

"Well, when's the next bus?" I asked.

"Not for another hour and a half," Jonathan said. "It's the weekend schedule." Jonathan paused for a moment. "Welp, I guess we'll just have to figure out something to do to amuse ourselves for the next hour and a half."

"Well, what the heck was the big rush all about then?" I asked.

Jonathan didn't answer. I was beginning to realize he had something up his sleeve. I didn't know what, but I figured whatever he had in mind was going right along according to plan. Jonathan finished up his hot dog, and we headed on up to the street. I had never walked around in New York City on my own before, but I wasn't exactly on my own since I was with Jonathan. The only times I had ever walked around at all in New York City had been on a few class trips to the museums, and once, I'd come with my parents to Radio City Music Hall. We'd never, on any of those occasions, walked down Forty-Second Street, which was right where Jonathan was headed. I wasn't exactly scared. It was more like I was excited, but I sure was glad I was with Jonathan, in more ways than one. The sidewalk was crowded, and there were lots of strange-looking people and also lots of mean-looking people. That was one of the reasons I was glad I was with Jonathan. Not necessarily because Jonathan could look so mean—he would have had a lot of competition in a meanness contest on that street—but because Jonathan was black. The black guys roaming around the street looked a whole lot meaner than anybody we ever saw down by old Roosevelt Field. I figured none of those guys would want to pick on Jonathan because there were plenty of unsuspecting, dumb tourist types who would be better targets, but still, I stuck as close to Jonathan as I could, which wasn't always easy. Jonathan loved to weave through the crowded sidewalks, and he seemed to know right where he was going.

In addition to all the strange people on Forty-Second Street, there was also a lot of really strange stuff. There were tons of movie theaters with all kinds of X-rated movies, and there were little shops with peep shows in them. I was hoping Jonathan didn't have any ideas about going into one of those peep shows, but sure enough, we stopped right in front of one.

"Now, the thing is," Jonathan said, "ya gotta act casual."

"What do ya mean?" I asked. "You're not thinking about actually going into one of these places!"

"Sure. Look. This kind of stuff is here, and we got to check it out," Jonathan said.

"Yeah, but they don't let kids into these kinds of places," I said.

"I know, dummy. That's why I said you got to act casual. The owners don't hardly know how old you are."

"But, Jonathan," I said.

"Look," Jonathan said. "The first thing you got to do is check out the magazines. You'll like them. Then we just slowly make our way down toward the back, where the peep shows are."

"But, Jonathan, you gotta be kidding."

We went in all right. The place was pretty crowded, so I didn't think anybody noticed us. We went over to the magazine rack, and Jonathan grabbed an X-rated magazine.

"Wow. Check this out," Jonathan said, and he showed me a picture of two naked people. "Come on. Grab a magazine," he whispered.

I grabbed one and started thumbing through it. It was pretty amazing, but I didn't want to look too enthused. Then Jonathan moved farther toward the back of the store. I stuck close. Then Jonathan nodded and whispered, "There's the peep shows."

I looked over and saw a long hall. It looked like there were a lot of closets down the hallway.

"You see," Jonathan said, "they got these booths over there, and you look through these peepholes, and you can see a live nude girl dancing around."

"Yeah?" I said. I must have said it too loudly because some guy from the front of the store started coming over. We both started thumbing through the magazines, and I tried my best to act cool, but I was scared.

"We don't allow no minors in here, boys," the man said.

"Well, we ain't no minors," Jonathan said. He was trying to act his meanest. "I'm eighteen, and so is my friend."

I was shaking too much to say anything.

"Well, let me see your driver's licenses," the man said.

"We took the bus," Jonathan said.

"Well, look. This ain't no library, boys. Buy what you want, and get out." The man was getting annoyed. I was perfectly content to do just what he'd said, but Jonathan was not satisfied.

"Yeah, well, I want to see the peep shows," Jonathan said.

"Well, ya gotta prove you're over eighteen for that stuff, bub," the man said.

"Dang! I said we took the bus," Jonathan said, using one of his meanest scowls ever.

I was getting more scared by the second.

"Look, I don't want to make no trouble," the man said as he put his grimy hand on my shoulder.

"Let's get the heck out of here," I told Jonathan, and I started toward the door.

"Okay, okay," Jonathan said. "Don't go causing a scene."

We pushed our way out to the street, and I was relieved to get out of there. However, my relief didn't last long, as I realized we were still on sleazy Forty-Second Street.

"Jonathan, let's get out of here," I said.

"But dang!" Jonathan said. "I still haven't seen a peep show."

We started back up Forty-Second Street, but Jonathan still wasn't done with his adventure. He still wasn't content.

"Look," he said. "This stuff is here, and we got to check it out. It's our duty as teenagers. Parents always try to hide stuff from us kids, so we got to go out and find out about it on our own."

"Yeah, but, Jonathan"—I was almost begging—"maybe the reason they don't want us to find out about this stuff is because it's no good."

"Bunk. It's just the opposite, ole boy. If it wasn't so good, they'd let us know about it right off the bat."

"Well, then maybe it's just too dangerous." I kind of understood what Jonathan was trying to say, but I was also darn sure that sneaking around Forty-Second Street wasn't the safest thing for two fifteen-year-olds to do. But Jonathan was bound and determined to expand his horizons, so our next stop was an X-rated movie theater to see a movie called *The Vixens*. The movie had started forty-five minutes before we arrived, but it would be too late to wait for the start of the other feature, *Stormy in Love*, so we paid three bucks—enough for a box seat at Yankee Stadium—and got in to watch a half-over movie.

We got to see stuff way far beyond anything in those magazines. The theater was real crowded and hot, and Jonathan went for some seats up close to the screen. We could hardly figure out what the movie's plot was, and Jonathan explained to me that plot didn't hardly matter in those kinds of movies. Pretty soon, some old fat guy in a dark coat sat down next to Jonathan. Then I heard a tiny squeal from Jonathan. I looked over at him, and I could see that his eyes were kind of bulging out of his head. At first, I figured it was because of what was going on in the movie, but then I noticed that the fat man next to Jonathan had his left hand on Jonathan's knee. Jonathan looked as if he were frozen solid, and I couldn't figure out if he was scared or kidding around or what. I gave him a little poke, but Jonathan didn't move a muscle.

I whispered, "Jonathan."

He still didn't move a muscle, and his eyes were still bulging out of his head.

Again, I whispered, "Jonathan," and he managed to move one of his eyeballs over toward me, but he didn't move any other part of his body. Boy, did Jonathan look strange. In the dark theater, with Jonathan's dark skin and dark face, just about all I could see was the white of his one eyeball, which was bulging out and kind of trying to look over at me.

I again whispered, "Jonathan," and I gave him a little poke.

Finally, he turned his head. Then he jumped up, walked right over me, and said, "He's a pervert. Let's get out of here!"

Jonathan pushed and shoved his way through the row, and when he got to the side aisle, he tore up it like crazy. I sure as heck wasn't going to be left alone in that dark theater with a pervert sitting near me, so I shot out of there and chased after Jonathan, who had stopped in the lobby.

"Well, what kept you? You like sitting next to a pervert!" Jonathan said. "Let's get out of here."

We bolted out the door and back into what we thought was the safe street, but of course, it was still old, slimy Forty-Second Street. It seemed like this time, even Jonathan had had enough.

"Well, have you finally had enough of this disgusting place?" Jonathan asked me.

"Why are you asking me? You're the one who said we got to see what's goin' on," I said.

"Yeah. Sure. Well, that was enough for me. I want to get home in time to see Disneyland," Jonathan said. "What do they call that show—*The Wonderful World of Color*? I really do like that name." Jonathan's sly, mischievous smile was back, and he started weaving through the sidewalk traffic at his usual breakneck speed. I tried my darnedest to keep up, but at least this time, we were headed back to the Port Authority.

I got home late, at about seven thirty, and I thought I was in for big trouble. Jonathan told me to say we'd missed the first bus and the next bus had broken down. He said that usually worked for him, but when I got home, the first thing my father said was "So you had to go and pick an extra-inning game for your first ball game without me. Your mother was worried sick, but I just told her how you and your brother always insisted on staying until the last out, even if a game went into extra innings."

I was surprised at what my father was saying, but I was no dummy, so I went along with it.

"Ah. Yeah. Sure. Wow! Extra innings!"

"That was some rally the Mets had in the bottom of the ninth," my father said.

"Ah. Yeah. Yeah! Wow! What a rally." *That must have been all the cheering we heard as we were leaving*, I thought to myself.

"You know, your mother made me watch the game to see if we could see you. Hey, and was that you guys way back there over by the third-base line?"

"Well. Ah. No. We had seats behind home plate." I was glad he was off the subject of the details of the game.

But then he asked, "How about that catch by Cleon Jones in the tenth inning?"

"Yeah. Ah. Wow! It was great. Wasn't it?"

"No, I mean it looked like on the television that he trapped the ball."

"Well. Ah. Yeah. Well, yeah. But we really couldn't tell." I was starting to have trouble faking it.

"Well, jeez," my father said. "You figure when you're at the game, you should be able to see better."

I started to sweat with nervousness. I still didn't even know who actually had won the game, let alone whether or not Cleon Jones had made a stupid shoestring catch or not. But then my good ole sweet mom came to the rescue with one of her good ole dumb questions, which I usually couldn't stand, but this time, I welcomed it.

"Were you cold out there today?" she asked. "It got a little nippy later this afternoon. You should have taken a jacket."

"Yeah. Ah. Well. Yeah! Yeah! You're right, Ma. It sure did get a bit nippy out there." Usually, I couldn't stand it when she started in with that stuff about taking a stupid jacket, as if I were still a dumb little kid, but this time, well, like I said, I was no dummy. I needed a change of subject, and I jumped at it.

"Yeah, you're right, Ma. I sure do wish I'd had my jacket today. Gee, what did the temperature go down to?" I was starting to feel like Jonathan pulling his Eddie Haskell routine. I could see Jonathan pulling the same thing with his folks at that very moment.

"Well, it sure got nippy," my mother said.

It seemed she wasn't quite ready to go on with the conversation, because she probably hadn't expected me to agree with her.

"Well, I'll remember next time," I said.

My father had kind of lost interest in the discussion by that time, so I was safe and headed up to my room. However, just as I started to go, my father caught me off guard with another question.

"And so what souvenirs did you buy?"

I was sure he was remembering all the times we hung around Yankee Stadium while I tried to decide what I wanted to get for a souvenir.

"Ah. Well. Um." I was stumbling a bit, but then the old mind came through in the clutch with a great answer. "Ah. Well. Hey! It was just a Mets game. What the heck would I want with a stupid Mets souvenir?"

"Oh yeah, that's right." My father nodded, and I was finally safe. I ran upstairs, clicked on my transistor radio, and waited for the baseball scores. I didn't want to take any chances.

I went to one other game with Jonathan last year—a Yankee doubleheader. There was a group of us that time, so my parents were not as concerned about my going to New York unsupervised by an adult, and since we'd lucked out with the Mets game, my parents had started to think Jonathan was a responsible adolescent. Our friend Phil was also coming, and since he had a well-deserved reputation as a studious and responsible young man—even though he was a Mets fan—we got the okay from our parents. That day, when we went to see the Yanks, the group consisted of Jonathan, Frankie, Phil, and me—and, of course, my stupid jacket.

It was the first non-adult-supervised game for Frankie and Phil, so Jonathan and I felt like big kids showing around the little kids, but of course, ole Jonathan took the lead. I didn't mind one bit because I hardly knew how to get to Yankee Stadium any other way than sitting in the back seat of my father's car, and getting to Yankee Stadium by bus and subway was a little more complicated than going to Shea. We had to take the bus to the Port Authority Bus Terminal, but from there, we had to walk through lots of underground tunnels to take one subway to one street and then get another subway to another street, and there weren't any easy blue arrows pointing the way like there were for Shea. But as usual, Jonathan knew exactly where he was going, and as usual, he was rushing ahead as if he were in a real big hurry to get some place real important, which wasn't so bad because we were all excited about going to see the Mick, and none of us had any problems about hurrying, except maybe Frankie, who had a way of falling behind. Frankie was always either staring at stuff, talking someone's ear off about something, or just generally not paying much attention to what the heck he was doing. So I'd be walking with

Frankie and trying to keep up with Jonathan, but Frankie would be talking a mile a minute about something, and then we'd start lagging behind, and we'd almost have to run to keep up with Jonathan.

Since it was a Sunday and the game was a doubleheader with the Tigers, it was pretty crowded in the subways. We could see that lots of people made it to the stadium without driving, but the crowds made it hard to keep up with Jonathan. Somehow, we made it, and when we emerged from the subway tunnel out onto the street, I couldn't help but ooh and aah when I saw the walls of the stadium. Whenever I saw it off in the distance from the car, it looked so big and white and stately, but this time, it just popped up right in front of us, and it was huge and amazing. I just gazed at it for a second—but only a second because Frankie grabbed ahold of my arm and said, "Come on. We gotta go catch up with that moron Jonathan." Sure enough, I could no longer even see Jonathan, but up ahead, Phil was motioning to us because he at least had a glimpse of Jonathan. We took off after Phil, who took off after Jonathan.

It was a great day. The sky was deep blue, and the grass was sparkling green. We had upper-deck box seats over on the first-base side. The Mick, who was playing first base because his legs were too worn out for center field, was having one of his all-time worst years. Some people, including Jonathan and Frankie, were saying he was washed up. At least Phil was content to stay nonpartial. The Mick managed a walk in the first inning, and then good ole Joe "the Nose" Pepitone hit a home run, and the

Yankees were in the lead to stay. Al Downing pitched a shutout, and the Yankees won 5–0. The Mick managed one single, so I was content, and since the game was never in jeopardy, they took him out in the seventh so he could rest up for the second game.

There was always so much to watch at a game. I always liked to watch the infielders warm up before the start of each inning. The Mick would throw each infielder a grounder. Well, actually, the Mick would never really throw a grounder. He would always throw each infielder a nice, easy one-hopper. I'd never know what good catching nice, easy one-hoppers was for the infielders, but the Mick always threw them exactly the same way. I watched him warming up the infielders in between innings throughout the entire doubleheader. Never once did he throw a practice grounder that took more than one bounce. I guessed it was just another talent the Mick had developed, since those days, all his other talents seemed to be fading. I was getting a little worried about the Mick. When the manager moved him to first base, everybody said he was getting a new lease on life, and it would extend his career, but last year, he had a pretty mediocre season, and this year, he was off to a real lousy start. It made me feel bad when people complained about how the Mick didn't have it anymore and said he should hang it up. I didn't believe it, and I sure didn't like hearing other people blabbering about it.

I loved doubleheaders. I couldn't see how anybody could want to go to anything but a doubleheader. One game just wasn't enough, and of course, if you didn't go to a doubleheader, you didn't get to see the groundskeepers working on the field in between the games. Everybody thought I was a weirdo for staying at my seat in between games to watch the grounds crew, but what the heck? What were they doing? Jonathan, of course, went to get a few more hot dogs. He'd already had two, and he said he was shooting for an even half dozen, but when he came back, he couldn't stop complaining about the line at the concession stand. Frankie had to go take a wicked piss, which he'd been moaning about since the seventh-inning stretch.

"I couldn't believe it," he said. "The line was longer than the friggin' line for the stupid hot dogs. And then when you got into the friggin' john, there was another line at each of the gall-darn urinals. I thought I was gonna burst. They should have it here like they used to have it at the old Polo Grounds. My uncle Vito once took us there to see the dumb Mets. And you should see the johns there. No stupid urinals. Just one big, long stupid trough that everyone gets to piss in at the same time. Just like pissing into a friggin' river. It was great! No stupid lines and no stupid urinals. Just a bunch of guys shoulder to shoulder with their weenies hanging out, doing their thing!"

Frankie went on and on about the bathrooms at the Polo Grounds until he almost made me have to puke—Frankie could be positively gross at times. Nobody ever found out where Phil went in between games, but Jonathan kept whispering to me that Phil was looking for a vendor that sold knishes, but Jonathan informed me that they only sold knishes at Shea Stadium.

I was content. I had already bought my peanuts and Cracker Jack from a vendor, so I just sat there and watched the grounds crew go about their business. They were smoothing out the dirt around home plate with rakes and lining the batter's boxes with a big wooden frame-type thing that looked like a window somebody had thrown out during cleanup week. The best job was driving the little cart that dragged the screen that smoothed out the infield dirt. The driver had to drive the cart carefully to make sure he didn't ever miss a spot. This driver was really good. Seriously. Around and around he went. From the first-base side to the third-base side, he carefully followed the cut-out part of the infield and never once accidentally drove over the precious infield grass or overlapped his previous work. While he was doing that, the other workers were busy smoothing out the pitcher's mound, changing the bases, and chalking the foul lines. It was really something to watch. When the cart driver was done, all the men got together and got a big, long, fat water hose. One guy got to water down the dirt just a bit so there was no dust. While he aimed the hose, the other men held the hose up so that it didn't leave a long dent in the grass. It was really something to watch, but almost everybody missed it because they were out buying hot dogs, going to the bathroom, or looking for knishes.

The second game started out really bad for the Yanks. In the second inning, the Tigers' pitcher, Hank Aguirre, who some said was the worst hitter the game had ever known, hit a triple with the bases loaded. Then the Tigers scored three more runs in the third inning, and it was looking pretty darn Bleaksville for the Bronx (used to be) Bombers. Then, in the fourth, the Mick led off and hit one of the longest balls I had ever seen. Yet because Yankee Stadium had such weird dimensions, all the Mick got was a ground-rule double. He hit the ball on a direct, solid line more than 440 feet to left-center field, where it was a ridiculous 457 feet from home plate to the wall. The ball took one bounce and hopped like a flash into the bleachers for a ground-rule double. It was one of the longest doubles in baseball history. Seriously. The Mick came around to score, and the Yanks eventually scrambled back to trail by one with a score of 7–6, and when the light-hitting Jake Gibbs, of all people, hit a game-tying pinch-hit home run in the ninth, we settled down for extra innings. What a bargain! We got not only two games for the price of one but extra innings to boot.

Well, the extra innings didn't work out too well. Good old fabulous Dooley Womack gave up a grand-slam home run to Dick McAuliffe in the twelfth inning, and the Yanks were losers. Losing was something they had been doing a little too much of those days.

We were a little sad as we left the stadium, except for Jonathan, who, being a Tigers fan, was pretty darn gleeful and off on one of his crazy zigzags through the crowd. We tried our best to stay with him, and we managed to make it down to the subway platform in record time. When we got there, I was a little pissed at Jonathan because I had wanted to stop for a Yankee yearbook and a few souvenirs, but ole Jonathan gave his usual line about not wanting to miss the next bus, and of course, Frankie couldn't help but blurt out something dumb while we were all jammed together in a crowd, waiting for a subway.

"I know why you're in such a hurry, Jonathan. You want to go see the peep shows. Yeah. Well, you can count me in." Frankie said it loudly enough so that everybody around could hear him. Some guy with his two kids, who were wearing their little Yankees caps and carrying their little baseball gloves, which they probably figured they could use to catch a foul ball or something—nobody told them they had a one-in-a-million chance of catching a stupid ball—grabbed his two kids and dragged them away from us.

Well, of course, Jonathan wouldn't let on to us what his real motive was, and we all jammed into the first subway. The subway was so crowded there was no way any of us could manage to get a seat. We were swaying back and forth in the subway car, and I was trying to check my score card, while Frankie was going on complaining about how crowded it was and how his feet hurt. Then he whispered to me that he couldn't wait to see a peep show but was kind of scared about roaming around on Forty-Second Street. I told Frankie that he was right to be scared of Forty-Second Street and that I had never seen more weirdos anywhere else in all my life. Frankie went on and on about how he wanted to see the peep shows because he wanted "to see it all," he said. Just then, some people got off, and a seat opened up. Frankie made a beeline for it.

"Wow. That's better," Frankie said, but now he was sitting a few feet away from me, so we really couldn't talk. As we pulled out of that station, I tried to see what street it was, but I couldn't make it out. Now that Frankie was out of earshot, I got back to checking my score card. I was trying to see where it had all gone wrong for my Yanks, but before I knew it, the subway was screeching to a stop, and I heard Jonathan calling for me.

"This is where we get off," he said. "Come on."

I just about panicked because I didn't think I'd make it to the door, and I pushed my way frantically through to the door and jumped out just in the nick of time. As I was breathing a sigh of relief, Phil asked me, "Where's Frankie?"

"What?" I said, and I realized I had forgotten about Frankie. I turned around, and as the train began to pull away, I saw Frankie banging on the door with a terrified look on his face.

"Frankie!" I yelled. "Oh my God! Frankie! You stupid idiot!" I turned to Jonathan. "Well, you really did it now, Jonathan, you moron! You're always in such a big hurry."

"Now, calm down," Phil said to me. "Look, Frankie will be all right. Won't he, Jonathan?"

"Sure," Jonathan said. "If he has any intelligence and knows the subways."

We all looked at each other and shook our heads. He was in big trouble.

"So, Jonathan, where in the heck are we now?" I asked.

"We're at Fifty-Ninth Street," he said.

"And so where is Frankie headed to?" I asked.

"Queens," Jonathan said.

"Queens!" I yelled. I tried not to get too emotional, but that statement really got to me. "Where in the heck is Queens?"

"Well, that's kinda like over where the World's Fair was—except the World's Fair and Shea Stadium are over in Flushing." Jonathan tried to be precise.

"Oh, that's really great," I said. "Poor dumb Frankie is going to be wandering around somewhere over in Queens, which is kinda like where Flushing is and kinda like where the World's Fair was and Shea Stadium is. Great."

"Well, let's not panic," Phil said. "Let's just hope Frankie will get off at the first stop and hop on the next train going in the other direction. How does that sound?"

"That's right. That's all there is to it. Simple," Jonathan said.

"Sure. Real simple," I said sarcastically.

We waited and waited. The subway station had pretty much cleared out from any of the Yankee Stadium crowd. It was very quiet until a train would come in. Then there would be the tremendously horrible noise of the train coming in and screeching to a stop. Some pretty ragged people would get off, and some pretty ragged people would get on, but there was no sign of poor old Frankie. After we'd waited for about forty-five minutes, Jonathan decided he was going after Frankie. It was a noble gesture, but Phil and I wondered what the heck we'd do in the meantime. Jonathan told us we'd have to hop on the next A train and take it down to the Port Authority Bus Terminal. Jonathan checked the bus schedule, and we saw that there was a bus leaving on the hour until midnight, and it was already eight thirty.

"Why don't you let us go with you?" I asked.

"No. I can travel better alone," Jonathan said.

"But I can't leave without Frankie," I said. "I'm not going."

"Yeah. But I kinda better go," Phil said meekly. "I've still got to study for a biology test tomorrow, and you know I've been doing pretty darn lousy in that class."

"Yeah, Phil, that'll be the day, when you do lousy in a course," I said sarcastically.

"But seriously, I really do need to hit the books," Phil said.

"So you'd better go," Jonathan said. "If you get on the next train, you can make it for the nine o'clock bus. And, T. J., you don't want poor little Phil to go off by himself."

"Well, I guess not," I said. Most people called me by my initials: T. J. "Oh, but I really shouldn't leave Frankie."

"Forget about Frankie," Jonathan said. "I'll take care of him. Poor Phil here needs somebody with experience to get him through the subways."

I knew old smart-aleck Jonathan was trying to psychologize me into thinking I'd be some sort of a hero if I went along with Phil. But he did have a point. It was getting late, there was no reason why all of us should go off looking for Frankie, and Jonathan was the only one of us who knew anything about the subways. Just then, the A train rolled in.

"Go on, you guys," Jonathan said.

"Yeah, well, all right," I said. "But you'd better find Frankie. And if you don't find him soon, you'd better call the cops. And I'll be waiting up for Frankie to call me when he gets home. And if he ain't home by midnight, you know his parents are going to be hysterical."

I kept going on until Phil grabbed me by the arm and dragged me into the subway car. We caught the nine o'clock bus and made it home by ten. I didn't let on to my parents that anything was wrong.

Jonathan and Frankie didn't let out the real story until almost two weeks later, when Frankie couldn't hold it anymore. He called me the night of the game at about one o'clock in the morning and made me speak to his parents about how he had gotten lost on the subway. They didn't believe Frankie's story and thought he'd been out carousing in the big city. Frankie was just starting to get a reputation for doing a lot of screwing around, and his parents were starting to get suspicious. As Frankie finally let out, his parents' suspicions were justified.

Frankie had done what none of us gave him credit for being able to do. At first, he panicked. "I almost went in my pants," Frankie said. But he just got off the train at the next station and simply hopped onto the next train headed in the opposite direction. He got off at the Fifty-Ninth Street station about a minute after Phil and I had left. Of course, old conniving Jonathan wasn't going to let that golden opportunity slip away. Frankie said he was relieved to see Jonathan, but he was surprised when he heard the first words out of Jonathan's mouth: "So you wanna see a peep show?" Frankie said that Jonathan figured they had the perfect excuse for coming home real late and not catching hell from their parents. They would say Frankie got lost on the subways and was wandering around for hours until the gallant Jonathan found him, and they both hurried home on the first bus they could make, which was the midnight bus.

They took the subway to Forty-Second Street and wandered around until they got to a peep-show place. Frankie went on and on about how cool he and Jonathan were and how they had no trouble getting to see a peep show. Then, of course, Frankie went into great detail about the peep show. It was such a detailed story that I knew Frankie couldn't be lying.

"Yep. We saw it all. Everything. Nothin' left to the imagination at a peep show." Frankie went on and on.

"But weren't you scared walking around on Forty-Second Street?" I asked.

"Was I scared? I was friggin' petrified," Frankie said. "There are more weirdos walking around there than I've ever seen in my whole life—and I once went to Los Angeles for a weekend with my uncle Vito! But gall dang. It sure was worth it!"

I had to admit I was a little envious.

"Yep. Nothin' left to the imagination in a peep show," Frankie said.

# CHAPTER 6

# The Revolt of the Golgi Bodies

Jonathan and I were in the same biology class. Mr. Hackney, one of the all-time most boring teachers in the entire universe, was the teacher. When we were just little kids, when my brother was about a year away from going into high school, all the big kids used to warn my brother about how boring Mr. Hackney's biology class was. Then my brother had Mr. Hackney, and he warned me, so when I got him, I was fairly well prepared, except Mr. Hackney turned out to be even more boring than everybody had said. But I was fortunate. Somehow, I got to sit next to Jonathan, and we got to sit at the last lab desk in the last row, over by the windows. I didn't know if anybody had prepared Jonathan for Mr. Hackney, but I kind of thought Jonathan knew what to expect.

For the first month of the year, Jonathan was at his blacknoser best, asking all kinds of dumb, boring questions that only boring old Mr. Hackney thought were interesting. Jonathan stayed under control and had Mr. Hackney thinking he was a model student. Even boring Mr. Hackney could appreciate a model student, especially when that model student was a black kid. With Jonathan pulling his blacknosing routine and Mr. Hackney at his boring best, the class was almost unbearable, until we got to the chapters on the cell. Now, I was sure some biologists or scientists somewhere thought cells were pretty interesting, but I thought cells were the most boring things in the entire universe. Learning about them from the most boring teacher in the entire universe was a brutal experience, except fortunately we had Jonathan in the class.

It all started when Mr. Hackney described the different parts of the cell. First, there was the cell membrane, which surrounded each cell like a wall. The cell was filled up with stuff called cytoplasm. Floating in the cytoplasm were all kinds of weird junk with some really weird names, like the Golgi body, ribosomes, the endoplasmic reticulum, and mitochondria. Right in the middle of each cell was the nucleus. Well, as Mr. Hackney was going through all this in his usual boring way, Jonathan said that he was going to start his own cell. He said he was going to be the nucleus, and then he started telling kids in the class that they could be parts of his cell. Of course, Jonathan would do this when Mr. Hackney was out of the room or before or after class. It took boring Mr. Hackney quite a few weeks to get through the chapters on the cell, and all the while, Jonathan was making up his own cell.

It was sort of like a club. The first thing you had to do to get into the club was pass through the cell membrane or cell wall, and of course, Jonathan was in charge of deciding who got through the cell wall. Once he let you through the cell wall, you had to float around in the cytoplasm for a while until you earned a higher position as a ribosome. Then came the endoplasmic reticulum, but if you were stupid or goofy or something, you got stuck being a lowly Golgi body. If you were really good, you got the highly respectable position of mitochondrion, and just maybe, if you were really good and thought of very highly by Jonathan, he'd let you into the nucleus.

Needless to say, when Jonathan started his cell, he was the only one in the nucleus. I considered myself fortunate to be an endoplasmic reticulum. Phil was assigned the position of ribosome, and everybody else was just floating around in the cytoplasm—except Mr. Hackney. Jonathan vowed never to allow Mr. Hackney through the cell wall. Jonathan decided that everybody in our biology class had to be considered in his cell. At first, nobody appreciated what an honor it was to be in Jonathan's cell, but soon the idea started to catch on. Some of the kids in the class wanted to know why they could only float around in the cytoplasm. When they found out that Phil was a ribosome and that I got to be an endoplasmic reticulum, they started to get pretty darn jealous. Then Jonathan started to develop a bunch of qualifications you had to meet in order to actually become a part of the cell and not just be floating around.

One guy, Harry, really wanted to be an endoplasmic reticulum like I was, but Jonathan told him, "No way." However, he promised Harry could be a ribosome if he wore a Groucho Marx mask to class one day—you know, one of those dopey pair of fake eyeglasses with the fake eyebrows, mustache, and nose. Well, Harry was normally a rather studious guy, but I guess Mr. Hackney's boredom really got to him, so he figured he'd try it. At least it would liven up the class, and maybe he could move up to ribosome. Well, Harry did it, and since he sat in the back of the room and Mr. Hackney's eyesight was pretty bad, Mr. Hackney didn't even notice. Of course, the whole class was snickering and laughing throughout the entire hour. One guy, Jimmy, asked a really complex question—we suspected Harry had recruited him to distract Mr. Hackney—and dumb Mr. Hackney tried for almost the whole class to answer the stupid question. All the while, Harry was sitting in the back with his Groucho Marx mask, totally unnoticed by Mr. Hackney. At the end of the class, Jonathan conducted a little ceremony in the hall, in which he not only promoted Harry all the way to endoplasmic reticulum but also promoted Jimmy to ribosome.

The next day, after biology class, Jonathan gave me a promotion to mitochondrion and moved up Phil to endoplasmic reticulum. After all, it was only fair since he had now promoted other people.

Those types of stunts started to become a regular thing in our class. Somebody would ask to be a ribosome or an endoplasmic reticulum, and Jonathan would devise some task he would make the person do to earn the position. It was usually something really ridulous that would crack up the class. Jonathan made one girl burp three times at specific times during class in order to be a ribosome. She did it. He made one guy hold three pencils in his teeth for an entire class to be an endoplasmic reticulum. He did it. Jonathan made another guy cough every two minutes to be a ribosome. He did it. He made one guy and girl sit through an entire class holding hands, with their hands on their desk, even though they couldn't stand each other, just to be ribosomes. They did it. He made one kid sit through the entire class with a Mets baseball cap on, and when Mr. Hackney asked him to take it off, he was required to say that his mother made him wear it because he had a head cold. Mr. Hackney let him wear the cap.

Eventually, just about everybody in the class did something to earn the status of a ribosome or endoplasmic reticulum. Jonathan also made four kids Golgi bodies. They were the kids in the class who wanted to move out of the cytoplasm but whom Jonathan couldn't stand. At first, nobody really knew that Golgi bodies were any different from ribosomes. Jonathan then set a deadline for all other kids in the class who were still floating in the cell to perform a certain task, or else they'd be squished through the cell wall and banished forever. Jonathan picked a date for each kid. He said that on that date, during Mr. Hackney's class, they were required to ask Mr. Hackney a simple question, and when Mr. Hackney answered it, they were required to say, "Sock it to me, baby," just like Judy Carne and Goldie Hawn did on the show *Laugh-In*. Now, it really wasn't a difficult task, but most of those kids were the smartest and most studious in the class. They hardly ever screwed around at all; all they ever did was answer the hardest questions Mr. Hackney asked and get an A+ on every test. However, even those kids agreed that Mr. Hackney was the most boring teacher in the entire universe. They realized what a horrible punishment it would be to be expelled from the cell, and they probably thought it might look bad on their record when they applied for college. So day by day, each one of the supersmart kids calmly—without much emotion and without laughing or anything—said, "Sock it to me, baby," to Mr. Hackney after he answered his or her question.

When the first kid said it, Mr. Hackney kind of raised one eyebrow and then ignored it, as if he hadn't heard anything. The rest of us were busting a gut trying not to laugh out loud. The next day, when another smart kid calmly said, "Sock it to me, baby," Mr. Hackney said, "Excuse me. What was that?"

The kid was super cool about it and just said, "Oh, nothing. I didn't say anything." Mr. Hackney kind of raised his eyebrow again but then went on with his lesson. Finally, when the last kid said it the next day, Mr. Hackney looked downright pissed off, and old Mr. Hackney was usually too boring to even get mad.

"What was that remark?" he asked sharply.

The girl who'd said it got real nervous and didn't know what to say, but Jonathan came to the rescue and, in his best blacknosing voice, said, "Excuse me, Mr. Hackney.

The young lady said, 'Sock it to me, baby,' which is a new slang term that the young adolescents are using these days to express praise for a job well done. She was merely trying to say thank you, sir, and well done."

Mr. Hackney stared at Jonathan and raised both eyebrows. Luckily, just then, the bell rang, and there was the usual confusion as everybody got up to head to the next class. Mr. Hackney just stood there at the head of the class with both eyebrows raised, kind of in a trance. Everybody got out of that class as quickly as possible because we were all splitting a gut trying to hold our laughter. The whole class was out of the cytoplasm and happy in their new roles as part of the cell. There were now nineteen ribosomes, five Golgi bodies, seven endoplasmic reticuli, and one mitochondrion, and of course, Jonathan was the nucleus. We were all just one happy cell until Jonathan found out that his cell's reputation had spread so far that kids from other classes wanted to get into the cell. Jonathan was faced with an entirely new dilemma.

Frankie was the first person outside of our biology class to express an interest in being in the cell. He said his class was studying the cell too, and he thought it would be totally neat to be part of a real live cell. Of course, Frankie always wanted to stick his nose into everything. I told him Jonathan controlled who was in the cell, so Frankie would have to ask Jonathan. Well, Frankie and about four other kids from Frankie's biology class did just that.

Jonathan got ahold of me and Phil and said he had a real serious problem. It was rare for Jonathan to be serious about any problem, but this time, he seemed genuinely concerned. Jonathan said that not only had Frankie and some of Frankie's friends asked to be in the cell, but some of his friends had too. He said this was a major policy question for the cell, and the whole future of the cell rested on his decision. Jonathan said he'd spent all night trying to make a decision, and after many hours of anguish, he'd decided he would have to do what any other modern American leader would do: appoint a committee to study the issue.

He decided he would put Phil and me on the committee, and in addition, he had made a truly momentous decision: he was going to allow Phil and me to go into the nucleus of the cell with him. At first, I thought the whole thing was pretty darn funny, but Jonathan was dead serious about it, so Phil and I just kind of said, "Yeah. Hey, sure. That would be an honor." Then Jonathan said that Phil and I would both be appointed to the second-highest position in the entire cell, the nucleolus. Our first assignment as members of the nucleolus would be to meet with Jonathan to decide how to allow outsiders into the cell—what qualifications we would require and what tasks the outsiders would need to perform in order to be admitted into the cell. Jonathan then scheduled a meeting of his nucleolus committee for lunchtime the next day in the school parking lot. Phil and I said, "Okay, fine." We both thought Jonathan was taking things a little too far, but then again, we both agreed it was quite an honor to be in the nucleus of the cell, even though I kind of liked being a mitochondrion.

When we had the meeting, I could see that Jonathan was dead serious again. He said that many momentous decisions had been made throughout the course of history—like when Lincoln freed the slaves, when the Japanese attacked Pearl Harbor, or when the Chicago Cubs traded Lou Brock to the Cardinals—and that some of those decisions were the right thing to do, like freeing the slaves, but some things hadn't turned out too well, like for the Japs attacking Pearl Harbor and especially for the Cubs trading Lou Brock. So he said we had better take some time to consider this problem and make sure we didn't do something we would regret.

I said that we should just let anybody in who wanted to get in, but then Phil said he thought we should be a little bit careful about who we let in. He said Frankie had been hanging out with some pretty weird people these days and we shouldn't let just anybody in. Jonathan suggested we devise an admission test, but I said that with a test, we'd be just like some stupid teachers. Who wanted to take any more tests? Jonathan then said that maybe we should just let anybody into the cell as long as the person was our friend and was taking biology. After all, someone in biology class would be able to appreciate what a cell was and would have had to spend all that time being bored studying it.

Then Phil suggested we let all our friends in, provided they were taking biology and were in the tenth grade. I said that they had to be going to our school, and Jonathan had one more requirement: all new members who entered the cell would be assigned the position of Golgi body. We all agreed it only made sense that if we allowed anybody through the cell wall, the person would have to start at the bottom as a Golgi body and work his or her way up. We didn't realize then that we might as well have decided to bomb Pearl Harbor.

Once we had our admission policy, Jonathan started letting more and more kids into the cell. Before he would let people in, he would make them study all the parts of the cell. The new applicants would then have to recite the cell parts according to their status in Jonathan's cell. He also made them say, "Sock it to me, baby," three times to their biology teacher. Another member of the cell would have to witness the kid saying, "Sock it to me, baby," or if that was not possible, Jonathan would grant a "Sock it to me, baby" waiver and instead make the kid wear a Groucho Marx disguise. All this stuff actually encouraged a lot of kids to join because most kids would use any excuse to do something stupid during school hours. Our membership grew and grew, or as Jonathan would say, the cell was expanding. The trouble was, we were being overrun by Golgi bodies. It seemed a lot of the kids actually liked being Golgi bodies at first because it was such a weird name. A lot of the guys liked to make jokes about the girls who were Golgi bodies. When some of the guys would walk by some of the good-looking girls, they'd say, "Now, there goes a Golgi *body*," with emphasis on the word *body*.

One day, as we went into biology class, Jonathan had a strange look on his face and told Phil and me in a serious voice that he wanted to meet with his nucleolus immediately after class. Nobody except teachers ever used the word *immediately*, so Phil and I figured it was pretty important. When we met in the hall, Jonathan looked strange. He kind of looked scared and was a little pale, which was a little hard for black kids, I guessed.

"My homeroom teacher said I have to go see the principal at ten o'clock," Jonathan said. "She said it has something to do with 'Sock it to me, baby' and Golgi bodies."

Phil and I started to crack up, but then Jonathan said, "Hey, wait a minute. This is serious. How did the principal find out about the cell? Hey, I could get in big trouble."

"Nah. Don't worry about it," I said. "He probably just wants to join." I laughed.

"Oh yeah. Thanks a lot. You're a big help," Jonathan said sarcastically.

"Hey, don't worry about it," Phil said. "You can handle it. You're the nucleus." Phil and I laughed, but Jonathan failed to see the humor.

"Thanks a lot," Jonathan said, shaking his head, and then he headed off down the hall.

Our next class was English. Phil and I went into English class without Jonathan, who headed to the principal. We couldn't have been sitting in class for more than ten minutes, when the messenger from the administration walked in and gave a note to our teacher. The teacher called Phil and me to her desk and gave us the note. We were to report immediately to the principal's office. We both gulped and walked out of the classroom.

As soon as we got out of the room, Phil kind of panicked, and he said, "Holy smokes! Jonathan probably blamed everything on us." He backed up against the wall and held his forehead.

"Well, now, let's not jump to conclusions," I said. "Maybe he's not even talking about the cell. Maybe he wants to congratulate you on your excellent campaign for class president."

"Aw, come on now. That was months ago," Phil said.

"Yeah. You're right. Maybe ..." I couldn't think of anything else to say, so we just headed downstairs. We figured we were already in enough trouble, so we didn't want to be late in reporting to the principal on top of everything else.

Our principal, Mr. Little, was a rather big guy, but nobody knew that because hardly anyone ever saw him. As a matter of fact, I didn't even know where his office was. He even had his own private secretary. His office was on the first floor, in the main hallway, not far from the auditorium. To get there, we had to go through the area known as "the office," where there were a bunch of secretaries who didn't do anything having to do with teaching. Most people said they kind of ran the school. Nobody was really scared of Mr. Little because we hardly ever heard of anybody going to see him. Mr. Krauzer was the guy everybody was afraid of—he was the detention officer. You usually didn't go to see Mr. Krauzer; he usually came to get you. Mr. Krauzer taught only one class all day, and the rest of the time, he was busy yelling at the kids the teachers were sick of yelling at. Mr. Krauzer did do one thing none of the others did: he stayed after school every day. It was part of his job. He ran the detention class, which met for one hour every day after school. Mr. Krauzer just stood there and looked mean for the whole hour, and he was pretty calm about the whole thing. He rarely even yelled during the hour. He just held on to his detention roster. If you said one word, he tacked one day extra onto the original detention punishment. I was only in detention once, but I had the misfortune of spending my sentence with Frankie. Jonathan's the one who got me in trouble, of course, and Frankie kept me in trouble once I got into detention.

You had to be pretty darn bad to get detention, and I honestly did not think I deserved it. I had the bad luck of being caught by Mr. Krauzer on a slow day when he was out looking for recruits for his after-school gathering. Jonathan had a brainy idea that we could steal all the chalk from Miss Stewart's class during lunchtime. He figured that if she didn't have any chalk with which to write on the blackboard, her ability to teach a class, which was already pretty limited, would be, in Jonathan's words, "further diminished." Miss Stewart's English class was our first class in the afternoon, so Jonathan figured we'd hang around a little in the halls after the morning classes and then sneak on over to her room, number 212, to steal all the chalk. The tricky part was that kids were not allowed to roam the halls during lunchtime. We were supposed to head to the lunchroom immediately or leave the building until a quarter after one.

Every lunchtime for about a week, Jonathan and I would take the long way to the lunchroom in order to go by room 212. One of us would stand outside on guard while the other one went into the room to steal all the chalk. It worked really well for a whole week. Miss Stewart would begin every class by fumbling around looking for the chalk, and then she'd get all frustrated and not know what to do. Then Jonathan would ask one of his stupid blacknosing questions, and he'd manage to waste most of the class. One day Miss Stewart didn't look for the chalk until just before she was going to give us our homework assignment, and she got so frustrated about not finding the dopey chalk that she forgot to give us the homework assignment.

Then came the day when old Mr. Krauzer caught me—not for stealing the chalk. Nobody ever figured out who did that, but he caught me in the hall well after the lunchtime period began. You see, after Jonathan and I completed our little thievery, we had to quickly head down to our lockers and then hurry on over to the lunchroom. Well, the time I got caught, I went all the way to the lunchroom but forgot that I needed some vocabulary words to study for Miss Stewart's class, so I headed back up to my locker, and on my way back to the lunchroom, I met old Mr. Personality, Mr. Krauzer. Well, he needed some recruits, and I looked perfect, so he nabbed me. I guessed that in a way, ole Miss Stewart got justice. Jonathan just said, "Justice will catch up to you white folks in the end. Us black folks got a lot of justice coming our way, so we can get away with this sort of stuff.

I bet even the Doc would agree." Jonathan liked to refer to Dr. Martin Luther King Jr. as the Doc, and he had a way of believing that his hero, Dr. King, would approve of all his shenanigans. I kind of doubted Dr. King would approve of anybody stealing chalk, but I thought he'd agree that I had gotten what I deserved and that Jonathan was just a bit luckier for not getting caught.

My one-day detention sentence turned into an entire week because I met Frankie there. Frankie was on the third day of a one-day sentence. He had a way of getting caught for doing something pretty dumb but harmless and then winding up stretching his detention out for more than a week because he could not ever sit for one hour without saying a word. With me sitting next to him, he couldn't help but try to talk to me. I'd try to tell him to pipe down, but old Mr. Krauzer would hear us. He'd put a check mark by our names and simply say, "One more day for our two gentlemen in the back." That happened for four straight days. Finally, Frankie was sick and was absent from school, so I was able to keep my mouth shut and finally finish my sentence.

When the secretary showed us into Mr. Little's room, Jonathan was sitting attentively in a chair opposite Mr. Little's big desk.

"Come in, gentlemen," Mr. Little said. Phil and I were both a tiny bit scared. We sat down and fidgeted. We didn't know what to say. Then Mr. Little said, "Well, Jonathan, so this is your nucleolus."

"Yes, sir," Jonathan said. "But they used to be other parts. Phil used to be an endoplasmic reticulum, and T. J.

used to be a mitochondrion. As a matter of fact, we seem to be quite low on mitochondria right now, but we're hoping to make promotions soon."

"I see," Mr. Little said, and he rubbed his chin. "Let me see now. You have all the different parts of the cell represented?"

"That's right, sir," Jonathan said. He was using his blacknosing voice.

"Well, now, being an ex–biology teacher …"

As soon as Mr. Little said that, Phil and I looked at each other with a little smile because it looked like, judging from the way Jonathan was going into his flawless blacknosing routine and being that Mr. Little was an ex–biology teacher, things might not turn out so bad.

"I still have an interest in the different parts of the cell. But tell me, Jonathan—what is all this about a cell wall?"

I thought, *Oh my God, is Jonathan going to tell the principal of the school that in order to get into the cell or be promoted in the cell, you have to do stuff like wear a Groucho Marx mask or say, "Sock it to me, baby"?*

"Well, you see, sir," Jonathan answered, "in order to get into the cell, you have to pass a simple quiz having to do with the biological makeup of the cell or the function of a part of the cell. For instance, ask T. J. what the function of a mitochondrion is."

"Well, T. J., you're on," Mr. Little said.

I was caught off guard by the question, but I sure as heck knew that a mitochondrion was the powerhouse of the cell, which was why I'd wanted to be a mitochondrion in the first place. "Um. It's the powerhouse of the cell, sir," I said.

"Excellent," Mr. Little said.

"You see, sir, that's one of the reasons why T. J. has made it all the way up to the nucleolus," Jonathan said.

"I see," Mr. Little said, "but what about all these Golgi bodies?"

"That's actually the entry-level position in the cell, sir. It's somewhat like starting out as a teacher. But if you're smart enough and work hard enough, you can move all the way up to the nucleus, or to be the principal, like you did, sir." Jonathan said this with his best blacknosing smile.

"Yes. Yes, I see," Mr. Little said with a kind of crazed gleam in his eyes. "Yes, I understand. In addition to being a learning experience for your members, your cell is like a metaphor for this school." Mr. Little stood up and made a sweeping motion with his arm. "Why, it's a metaphor for the entire country!" he exclaimed.

I didn't think even Jonathan knew what the heck old Mr. Little was talking about.

"Well, Jonathan and boys, I think you've got quite an idea here. I think we should sanction your club as an official school club. That will give it the same status as the Spanish club, the glee club, or the technicians' club."

I was starting to think this was more than even Jonathan had hoped for.

"Then you can conduct meetings. Maybe even have an outing. What an excellent way to learn about biology. I should have thought of something like this myself when I was a teacher. Why, we could even have trips to museums and maybe even a trip to the university lab."

We were all starting to get a little worried, and then Mr. Little really floored us. "And of course, you'll need an adviser. I think I'll appoint Mr. Hackney."

"Oh no! No," Jonathan said. I could see that Jonathan was pretty upset, but he tried to do his best to remain calm. "Um, no. That won't be necessary. Ah. You don't have to inconvenience Mr. Hackney. He's already done enough for the cell."

"Don't be silly, young man. A club must have an adviser," Mr. Little said.

"Yeah. But that'll be okay. We really don't need an adviser," I blurted out. I couldn't sit back in silence any longer.

"Yeah, that's right. We don't need an adviser," Phil added.

"Hmm." Mr. Little rubbed his chin thoughtfully. "I think I know what you're trying to say. Old Clarence— Mr. Hackney—is somewhat boring, isn't he? Well, I'll tell you what. Yep. I know exactly what I'm going to do."

We were all really worried now.

"I'll be your adviser!" Mr. Little said as he slapped both hands on his desk.

The three of us simultaneously said, "But—"

"Sure. I've been dying to get out of this old, stuffy office and back out there with my students."

"But, Mr. Little, you're much too busy with running the school to be an adviser for a club." Jonathan tried his best blacknosing, but I could see that this time it was not going to work.

"Nonsense, Jonathan," Mr. Little said. "I've got a little secret to tell you. Those secretaries out there actually run this school. I just sit in here and sign papers. It will be great to get out there again and work hand in hand with my students. Hey, I used to be a biology teacher. It will be great to get back to my favorite subject."

For the first time ever, Jonathan could not think of anything to say. We all just sat there in bewilderment.

"I think we'll have our first meeting next week," Mr. Little said. "Do you young fellows agree to that?"

We were all too stunned to say anything. Phil kind of nodded, so Mr. Little said, "Good. Good." He clapped his hands together and said, "Well, it's done. You boys had better get back up to class. Don't forget—next Tuesday at three fifteen."

We all got up to leave, but just before we left, Mr. Little said, "One more thing, boys. What's this about 'Sock it to me, baby'?"

Jonathan might have been shocked by that question, but he made a quick recovery. "Sir, it means something like 'Well done' or 'Thanks for telling me that.' It's black slang. Something black people used to say down on the plantation during slave times. It's part of black heritage."

"I see," Mr. Little said, and as we walked out of the room, Mr. Little followed us. He was still sort of excited by the whole stupid thing, and he said, "Well, fellows, sock it to me, baby!"

Jonathan turned around and said, "Yeah. Right. Right on. You got it."

We all hurried out past the secretaries, who were looking back at Mr. Little in disbelief.

There was one thing that no high school kids liked: the officially sanctioned clubs. When it came to extracurricular activities, you were either on one of the sports teams or in one of the school's lame bands. If you were a girl, you were a cheerleader or a twirler or in the color guard or the band, and that was it. There was other stuff for the seniors, like the yearbook staff, and there were always the class officers, who just ran for office and then planned a dance or something. Finally, there were all the lame officially sanctioned clubs disliked by everybody.

My brother once told me as a word of advice that I should join as many of the lame clubs as possible because activities looked good on applications for college. He said that colleges looked for stuff like that. It made them think you weren't some kind of deadbeat throughout your years in high school. He told me that he was in Spanish club for four years and they had exactly one meeting each year. That was it. They were supposed to speak only Spanish during the meetings, so whenever there was a meeting, nobody could understand what was going on. When they wanted to say something, if they couldn't think of how to say it in Spanish, they couldn't say it. Consequently, nobody ever had any good ideas in the Spanish club. If someone did have a good idea and figured out how to say it in Spanish, nobody else could understand him or her. The Spanish club adviser, Senor Alvarado, made sure nobody spoke any English. My brother said the only good thing that ever happened in Spanish club was that they once had a taco party. They were supposed to make their own tacos, but the kid who was supposed to bring the cornmeal for the tacos got confused and brought a dozen cans of Green Giant Niblets corn instead. Mr. Alvarado said there was no way they had enough time to grind out the Green Giant Niblets corn into cornmeal, so he went out and bought a dozen bags of tacos from the Jack in the Box fast food restaurant.

I wondered what the colleges would think when I put on my application that I was a member of the cell. Phil said they might think it was surreptitious—whatever the heck that meant. I wondered if I should put down that I was in the nucleolus. Would they be impressed?

Well, I was not quite sure why—maybe lots of kids knew of my brother's advice, maybe they just wanted to see what Mr. Little looked like, or maybe some of the kids had heard about Mr. Little saying, "Sock it to me, baby," and wanted to see if he would do it again—but there was an amazing turnout for the first meeting of the cell.

Mr. Little said that this was the founding meeting of the cell. He had Jonathan sit at the front of the room with me and Phil on either side. Mr. Little started the meeting with a long speech about how momentous this meeting was, how exciting it was to found a new club, how he'd been at the founding of the technicians' club back in 1952, and all kinds of stupid stuff like that. It was a boring speech. Finally, he turned the meeting over to Jonathan, the nucleus. Now, old Jonathan was no dummy. He knew he had a good thing going, and he sure didn't want to blow it. As the nucleus of a new club, he finally had what he called a power base. Jonathan was still pretty upset about losing the election for class president, and after all, Jonathan's ambition in life was to become president of the United States, so he figured that being the nucleus of the cell would be as good a way as any to start his ascent to power.

Jonathan told me later that in order to consolidate his power base, he needed to immediately win over his constituency. He said that Dr. Martin Luther King Jr. did it by organizing boycotts and Bobby Kennedy did it by criticizing LBJ. Jonathan said you had to give the people what they wanted, or else you lost their support. He knew that almost all the people in that room were there because they either thought the cell provided them a way to do stupid things while suffering through biology class or figured they might hear Mr. Little say, "Sock it to me, baby." Jonathan figured the chances of Mr. Little again saying, "Sock it to me, baby," were almost nil, and he knew that soon the novelty of being a part of the cell would wear off. He knew he had to get things going the right way and then keep his constituency interested, so he decided the best strategy would be to plan a party.

Everybody liked to have parties, and every officially sanctioned club was allowed to have a party or an event on school property. There was no need to waste any time. We figured we might as well start planning right then for a party. Now, Jonathan was not only smart but also shrewd. He knew that if he wanted to start planning for a party right off the bat, the suggestion would have to come from one of the members, not Jonathan. It might look bad otherwise, as if Jonathan, the head of this newly sanctioned official club, was more interested in having a party than promoting the educational benefits of having a bunch of students running around thinking they were parts of a cell. So Jonathan told his friend Killer, a newly inducted Golgi body, to suggest that we celebrate the club's founding with a gala cell party. It sounded pretty funny to hear Killer say the word *gala*, but it worked. Good old Mr. Little thought having a gala cell party to celebrate the founding of a brand-new officially sanctioned club was a grand idea. He said he wished somebody had thought of that way back in 1952 at the founding of the technicians' club.

As with most things, Jonathan was right, and the idea of having a gala cell party was all anybody talked about for the rest of the meeting—and for the next month, for that matter. Once the word got around, our entire grade wanted to join the cell just so they could go to the gala cell party. Much to Jonathan's dismay, we had to lower our admission standards to accommodate everyone who wanted to get in. We cut out the "Sock it to me, baby" requirement and the Groucho Marx masks and instead just gave each new applicant a simple test about the structure of the cell. Some of the kids were disappointed they didn't have to say, "Sock it to me, baby," but mostly, everybody wanted to be in on the gala cell party. Eventually, Jonathan had to call an emergency meeting of the nucleolus to figure out how we were going to accommodate all our new members. Jonathan said he didn't think it was healthy to have any cell overrun with Golgi bodies. He said it seemed like the cell wall was crumbling and the cell was being invaded. Then Phil said that if we didn't do something soon, our cell would become cancerous. Phil said that was how real live cancer worked—a bunch of cells grew wildly out of control. Well, if that was how cancer worked, we were having a cancer epidemic. Jonathan said all we could do was ride it out until after the gala cell party, at which time interest would be bound to subside.

We were also having problems with our arrangements for the party. Since we now had so many members, there was no way the school could put up enough money for a big enough party, and since the cell was so new, we hadn't even started to collect dues or have a fund raiser. Mr. Little, in his brilliant advisory capacity, came up with the wonderful suggestion to sell tickets for the party. He said that was the only way we'd ever be able to have a decent party. Jonathan said he didn't like the idea of selling tickets, because he was afraid that selling tickets would make the enthusiasm for the cell fizzle. Jonathan was still concerned about consolidating his power base.

"Well then," our fabulous adviser said, "why don't you charge a different amount per ticket according to the person's position in the cell?"

"Oh, I don't know about that," Jonathan said. He looked worried.

"Well, fellows, look," Mr. Little said. "You've got to sell tickets one way or the other. However you decide is up to you."

Then Mr. Little said he had to go sign some papers, and he left. Phil said, "Well, look, Jonathan. It doesn't seem like such a bad idea. We could charge some of the newer members a dollar more. They want to be in so bad they won't mind. And they didn't even have to do hardly anything to get into the cell. If they don't want to pay, well, we still have plenty of other members."

Then I had to open up my big mouth with my brilliant idea. "Yeah," I said. "Why don't we charge two dollars to all Golgi bodies and one dollar to everybody else? That would be a nice, organized way to do it."

"Yeah, real nice," Jonathan said. "But what'll our Golgi bodies say? You know any Golgi bodies?"

"A few," I said.

"Well, they might get pretty pissed off," Jonathan said.

*Pissed off* was hardly the term for it. When we put up the signs advertising the gala cell party, which stated that all members of the cell would be charged one dollar except for Golgi bodies, who would be charged two dollars, we faced more than a bunch of pissed-off kids. We faced a revolution. Of all people to rise up the ranks to leader of the revolution was my good buddy Frankie, who refused to even look at me after the signs went up. Another leader of the revolution was one of Jonathan's best friends, Lonnie, who was now pissed at Jonathan. Some of the kids started to carry signs that said, "Equal Rights for Golgi Bodies,"

"Golgi Bodies Shall Overcome," and "Resist." Worst of all, Frankie and Lonnie banded together and started a movement to boycott the gala cell party. Then they started a movement to overthrow the nucleolus. In the midst of this crisis, Jonathan's solution was to call for an emergency meeting of the besieged nucleolus.

We invited our adviser, Mr. Little, but he said he couldn't attend because he had other important appointments. We could see that Mr. Little's enthusiasm for the cell had already diminished, so it was up to us to try to figure a way out. Jonathan said he felt we were better off without Mr. Little because it was his advice that had gotten us into the mess in the first place. We had to hold the meeting in secret down in Jonathan's basement. After much debate, we decided to raise the ticket price to two dollars for everybody. The next day, we changed all the signs. The revolt of the Golgi bodies seemed to calm down, but soon enough, there was a backlash from the other parts of the cell, who complained that the Golgi bodies had caused a rise in ticket prices for everybody. A group called the Coalition of Concerned Ribosomes was formed. They felt that Golgi bodies should be charged more since Golgi bodies were, well, Golgi bodies. Another group called themselves the Citizens for a Safe Cell and called for the banishment of all Golgi bodies and for a reinforcement of the cell wall. The two groups then joined forces and called for a boycott of the gala cell party. Jonathan, of course, called for another emergency meeting of the nucleolus.

Mr. Little was away on business more and more those days, so he wasn't around for that meeting either. We decided at the meeting to lower the price for all members of the cell to a dollar. That seemed to make everybody happy—until the night of the gala cell party.

The party was held in the gym, and as school parties went, it started out as good as any. In fact, it was a heck of a lot better than most of the parties held by the officially sanctioned clubs. There was a band that did some Beatles songs and even tried to do stuff by The Temptations. We had plenty of food and lots of decorations. The decorations were extremely weird because they were made to look like parts of the cell, including ribosomes, endoplasmic reticuli, and mitochondria. It all looked pretty accurate according to pictures from the biology books. But then again, decorating the whole side of a gymnasium with ribosomes was strange. A huge cardboard mitochondrion hung from one of the backboards. The centerpiece was a green blob of stuff that was supposed to be the nucleolus. Phil told me that the crazy artist Andy Warhol would probably really appreciate the decorations. Of course, that was before the trouble started.

Jonathan was just about to pick the king and queen of the cell, when we heard some yelling over in the far corner of the gym. Nobody was sure who had started the argument, but it looked like it was turning into an argument between a Golgi body and a ribosome. Then other Golgi bodies came to the defense of the one Golgi body, and a bunch of ribosomes came to the defense of the ribosome. Well, soon some endoplasmic reticuli joined up with the ribosomes, and some mitochondria took the side of the Golgi bodies. Then somebody started throwing food, and soon there was an all-out food fight. They started throwing around pieces of scenery too, so there were chunks of mitochondria and pieces of ribosomes flying all over the gym along with bologna sandwiches and Fritos. It was full-scale biological warfare. The combatants were destroying everything. They started tearing away at the nucleolus structure. Finally, Mr. Little tried to come to the rescue; he grabbed the microphone from the band singer and started yelling for everyone to calm down. But nobody was about to listen. Then Mr. Little got hit with a piece of mitochondrion scenery with a little mustard on it, so he gave up and hid over with the band.

It looked like the fight was going to go on forever, until Jonathan got another one of his brainstorms. We were huddled under the remains of the nucleolus structure, when Jonathan got the idea that if he could get Mr. Little to say, "Sock it to me, baby," and get a bucket of water thrown in his face, maybe the kids would stop fighting to watch their principal be humiliated. Jonathan sent Phil out to get Mr. Little, who was hiding behind the bass player, and he brought Mr. Little with us into what Jonathan was calling the command bunker. I figured Jonathan felt that if he was going to be the president and the commander in chief of our armed forces someday, then this would be a good place to start using military lingo. He explained his plan to Mr. Little, who shook his head and ran his hands through his thinning gray hair. Jonathan told Mr. Little that he was our only hope and then tried to butter up old gullible Mr. Little with stories about heroic acts by great Americans, such as Teddy Roosevelt and the Rough Riders and John F. Kennedy and the PT-109, and then of course, he had to throw in Bob Gibson and his performance against the Yankees in the 1964 World Series. I gave Jonathan a glare because he knew the '64 World Series was a sore spot with me.

Mr. Little proved to be more gullible than I thought, and he bought the bait hook, line, and sinker. "Well, I guess somebody has to do something," he said with a stiff upper lip.

I went to get a bucket of water, but Jonathan whispered to me to take along Phil and get as many buckets of water as we could. Phil and I went out to the nearest slop sink, ducking flying pretzels, bowls of onion dip, and strawberry-ice-cream-covered endoplasmic reticuli along the way. When we got back, each with two buckets of water, Jonathan was at the microphone with Mr. Little alongside him. There was a spotlight on them. Jonathan had the drummer play a drumroll.

"Ladies and gentlemen," Jonathan said, "and Golgi bodies of all ages, your principal has something important to say to you."

The fighting subsided a bit, and a few kids looked over. I gave a bucket of water to Jonathan. Mr. Little stepped up to the microphone and yelled, "Sock it to me, baby!" *Wham!* Jonathan threw the pail of water at Mr. Little. Some of the kids were watching, but most of them were still throwing around Kraft American cheese slices and bits of ribosomes. Then Mr. Little yelled again,

"Sock it to me, baby!" Jonathan threw another pail of water at Mr. Little. Some of the kids stopped fighting and cheered. I raced out for two more buckets of water. Just before I got into the hall, I heard Mr. Little say, "Sock it to me, baby!" again, and there went another pail of water. The kids started cheering more. Finally, after nine shouts of "Sock it to me, baby!" and nine buckets of water, all hostilities ceased, and the partygoers gave Mr. Little a standing ovation.

Ole Mr. Little had saved the day. He was a hero—pretty darn wet but a hero. He told us that things were a lot different in the days of the founding of the technicians' club, back in 1952, when that guy Ike was elected president. According to Mr. Little, back then, things were a whole lot simpler.

CHAPTER 7

# Roosevelt Field, Darrell, and the Hawk

The JV practice field, Roosevelt Field, wasn't all that bad when you came right down to it. It had an all-dirt infield that was nothing to write home about, but it had a pretty sturdy backstop, and the outfield was basically flat. There was a street right out beyond the visitors' bench, and there were a few dumpy factories out on the other side of the street. Down a ways was the headquarters of the White Brothers Garbage Company.

I thought White Brothers was a strange name because every single person who worked on the trucks was black. I was kind of fascinated by the sight of all those garbage trucks parked at the big old White Brothers garage. I had been seeing those trucks for years, and I never knew where the heck they came from. In fact, the first black person I ever saw was driving one of those garbage trucks. When I was a kid, I didn't know that black people were anything but garbage men. On the other hand, I didn't know that garbage men could be anything else but black, until a couple of years ago, when I saw some news reports about some of the garbage men in New York City, and most of them were white guys. I was always amazed by how those garbage men rolled those big green garbage barrels up and down everybody's lawn. They'd spin the top of the barrel around and tip it at just the right angle so that the barrel would roll along real nice and not stand up straight or fall over. Then they'd go over to a house's garbage cans, dump them out into the barrel, roll the barrel to the garbage truck, and dump the garbage in the back. All of us kids who were up early on a Saturday morning would gather around the truck for the best part: one of the garbage men would pull down a lever; the truck would start whining; and the big old metal crusher would slowly come out, grab all the garbage, and jam it into the back of the truck. We were only little squirts, but we thought the garbage trucks were great. The best part of all was when one garbage man would hop onto the back of the truck and grab hold, and the truck would drive away with him just kind of hanging out there, having a great old time. Boy, I thought it would be great to be able to jump onto that truck and hang on with one hand while riding through the neighborhood—and to be able to twirl the garbage barrel with one hand and pull the magic lever to start the big old crusher. I thought garbage men were great.

One time, when I was still real little, some of my aunts and uncles were over, and my uncle Freddie asked me what I wanted to be when I grew up. I said with a whole lot of little-kid pride and sincerity that I wanted to be a garbage man. All the grown-ups started to laugh like crazy, and I felt really stupid and embarrassed. Then my uncle Freddie said, "You don't want to be like them coloreds, do you?" Everybody laughed again. I wasn't sure what he meant because I had never heard the word *colored* before, but I thought they were making fun of me, even though I didn't know why. I felt bad and snuck up into my room.

Later that day, my brother told me that the next time somebody asked me what I wanted to be when I grew up, I should just say I wanted to be a baseball player, which he said was what all dimwitted little boys were supposed to want to be when they grew up. I figured that was good advice because I really did want to be a baseball player back then. Then my brother said, "Oh, and don't tell them you want to be like Elston Howard." I wasn't sure what he meant by that, but I guessed it had something to do with the fact that Elston Howard was black.

As we started throwing that first day at Roosevelt Field, I still wished I had had a chance, just once, to pull that lever to start the garbage crusher.

It was nice to be practicing on good old grass and dirt instead of asphalt, as we could slide into bases, dive for ground balls, and get all dirty and have a great time. One of the great things about playing high school sports was that you could get real dirty and be proud of it. When my friends and I were kids, we always had a natural inclination toward getting dirty, and of course, our mothers were never too keen on dirt, so when we were out playing and having a great old time, in the back of our minds, we knew we were going to be yelled at for having a good time and getting filthy. However, most of us did it anyway and accepted the fact that we'd catch hell as soon as we went home for supper. It seemed there was some kind of rule that the amount of punishment you had to endure was directly related to the amount of fun you had.

I used to love to make headfirst slides into third base just like Yogi Berra did. The Mick was too cool to make headfirst slides, and he was also too fast to ever need to make a dopey headfirst slide. But Yogi was getting a little old, and he was pretty slow, so he would always make headfirst slides into third base. Well, when I started doing it, I had a number of things to consider. First of all, my idol was the Mick, so I sure as heck didn't want to go imitating old weird Yogi, but I had to admit that it was more fun to slide into third base headfirst than feetfirst. However, there was another thing to consider: when you slid into a base headfirst, you got twice as dirty as you did from a normal slide. Not only did you get your pants dirty, but you got your shirt, face, arms, and hands dirty. You got dirt in your hair, in your ears, and down your pants. So if getting dirty was your thing—and of course, most of us kids loved to get dirty—then the headfirst slide was the way to go. You could get dirtier with one headfirst slide than with a whole afternoon of playing with cars in the dirt.

Then again, there was another factor to consider: the punishment factor. Since the headfirst slide had twice the dirtying power of the normal slide, it therefore had twice the punishment potential. The punishment potential was directly proportional to the amount of fun we had, and the headfirst slide was way more fun. Naturally, I developed a sensational headfirst slide technique that old Yogi would have loved and even the Mick might have appreciated. But of course, my mother definitely did not appreciate it. "Did you have to bring half the dirt from the field home with you?" she'd say. Then she probably wouldn't let me go out after supper or something. But what the heck? You had to learn to compromise. In order to do one thing, you had to give up another, and there was no way I was going to give up the old headfirst slide.

However, as I got older, a funny thing happened: there were a few things I didn't have to compromise on any longer, and one was the headfirst slide. The first time I pulled my headfirst slide in practice, my coach went crazy—crazy with praise!

"What a great effort," he said. "That's what I want all you guys to do. Put out that extra effort every second. If I catch any of you loafing or not putting out one hundred ten percent, you'll be catching splinters on the bench. When you slide, slide hard and fast. When you go after a ball, go after it all out. Dive if you have to, but give it all you've got."

In other words, he was saying, "Bring home half the dirt from the field with you." It was a license to get dirty! All of a sudden, getting dirty was praised, not punished. A dirty uniform was something to be proud of—a status symbol—and I was great at getting dirty. Of course, my mother was still in charge of washing my uniform, so I still had to hear, "Did you have to bring half the dirt from the field home with you?" But at least I got to go out after supper.

By the time we were scheduled for our first scrimmage, I was in a fight for the starting shortstop job with a black kid named Darrell. Darrell was from Roosevelt School, and he was kind of what everybody expected a black kid to be like. He wasn't a bad kid or anything, though he had been kicked out of school twice already for fighting, and rumor had it that the highest mark Darrell had ever gotten in a class was a D+—and that was in gym. Darrell was the only person I knew who could make a mean face that rivaled one of Jonathan's scowls. Even Jonathan admitted he'd like to learn some of Darrell's meanness techniques. Of course, Jonathan was just putting on an act, and Darrell wasn't. Darrell seemed to be mean right down to the core. He wasn't too good of a ballplayer, but he played hard—not out of fun or dedication but, as Jonathan would say, out of pure oppressed-black-person meanness.

Darrell had a following. Most of the other black kids on the team respected him. They weren't quite sure what to make of Jonathan, but there were no mysteries about Darrell. Darrell seemed to be like all the black kids from Roosevelt School, only a whole lot meaner.

I was beginning to have more and more trouble with my throwing, and my coach was getting on my case more and more. Darrell didn't have my consistency at catching grounders, but he had a strong and accurate arm. The other players started calling him the Rifle, and I was still the Wrecker. I was having particular troubles with my coach because he insisted that I learn to throw overarm. It wasn't an unreasonable request, and he was the coach, but I had never really thrown overarm in my whole life. I didn't know why. I just naturally threw sidearm. Of course, when you threw the ball sidearm, a funny thing happened on the ball's way over to first base: it sort of curved a little. It faded out a little over to the right. I'd always had some trouble controlling my sidearm throws, but I'd always been able to compensate a little by aiming over to the left a little more, and then the ball would fade on over to its target. However, that wasn't good enough for the coach. He wanted us to throw overarm. It was overarm or nothing. So I tried overarm—and I threw worse. Then I'd sneak in an old familiar sidearm throw, but I'd forget to compensate for the curve, and the throw would go sailing away. Then I'd catch hell from the coach. So I'd try to throw overarm again, and I'd never know where the heck the ball was going to go. Then I'd catch more hell. I was getting pretty worried. I lost all confidence in my throwing, and when someone lost his confidence, he was going to lose his job, and he might as well find a seat on the bench, which was where I was headed. By the first scrimmage, Darrell was the starting shortstop, and I was on the bench. I really needed somebody to bolster my confidence, but of course, Frankie was gone, and I was only left with Jonathan, who had to try not to be too chummy with me so as not to antagonize Darrell's buddies.

Then the coach started to criticize my switch-hitting. Nobody had ever bothered me before about my switch-hitting. Old Mr. Gonzo had seemed to think it was rather neat that one of his players was a switch-hitter just like the Mick, but the JV coach didn't go for it. He said I was too young to switch-hit, and besides, I really couldn't hit lefty anyway. He was correct about that, but I could still bunt, and I had learned how to slap the ball to left field. It looked a little funny, but when I batted lefty, I'd wait on the ball a real long time to get a good look at it, and then I'd slap the ball to left field and almost always get a hit. Lefty hitters were really rare in high school; there were far more righty hitters than lefties. That was why coaches always put their worst fielders out in right field. When a lefty hitter would get up, everybody'd yell, "Lefty! Lefty!" as if everybody had been suddenly struck with blindness. Then all the fielders would shift over toward right field— of course, nobody ever pulled this shift when a righty batter came up. So whenever I got up to hit lefty, all the fielders would naturally shift a bit over to right, and I would slap a little grounder or hit a little blooper to left and get a sure hit. But that didn't matter because the coach didn't like switch-hitters.

Now, I wasn't much of a hitter when hitting righty, but I could swing the bat a little harder, and I didn't look as awkward, so the coach told me to work on my righty hitting. I knew as well as anyone how well I could hit righty—not well at all. I got a few hits and occasionally hit a long fly, but in order to be productive at the plate, I needed to slap a few hits lefty or at least drag a bunt single.

However, the coach wouldn't hear of it. I was to learn to bat righty or nothing—no Mickey Mantle kid stuff up there in JV. I was to learn to throw overarm and learn to bat correctly, one way. I'd known things were gonna be different, but I sure wasn't prepared for that.

March was a tough month for baseball. We all really wanted to get out and play since we were sick of winter, but unfortunately, it could get pretty darn cold and windy in March. Jonathan referred to the cold wind in March as the hawk.

"The hawk's really biting today," Jonathan would say, and then we'd try to take batting practice, and our hands would sting every time we made contact with a pitch. It kind of made me happy when I swung and missed. I'd stand up there with the stupid wind swirling around, and I'd get dirt in my eyes and have to squint, but the coach would expect the players to be hitting vicious line drives somehow. It was almost as bad when I got out in the field. I had enough trouble trying to throw the ball straight without the wind making things even more difficult.

We had one stretch of cold gray days that I thought would last forever. There was no sun in sight all week—no warmth all week. By the end of the week, I was praying for it to rain or snow so practice would be canceled. I never thought I'd actually wish for rain to cancel an opportunity to play baseball, but that was how I felt. When Friday rolled around, there was a slow, constant drizzle. It was cold, gray, and wet, and the hawk was biting but not bad enough for the coach to cancel practice. I was sure he never even considered it. So there we were, standing around, just about freezing to death, with the coach taking us through his drills. First, we did wind sprints. Then we did some ridiculous calisthenics. Then we did some throwing to loosen up our arms, which were hardly going to warm up because they were half frozen. Then came infield practice. We had to whip the ball around, and each time we'd catch a ball, our hands would sting like crazy. Then we did some batting practice, and of course, the coach wouldn't let me switch-hit anymore, so I had to bat righty all the time. Since I was a pretty lousy hitter anyway, batting practice was a real ordeal. Things were different from freshman year all right. This coach played to win, and his attitude was "Practice, practice, practice. Work, work, work," hawk or no hawk.

The number-one worst part of those cold gray March days was going home alone. After such a lousy practice, I should have been happy to get out of there and head home, but I wasn't. It wasn't so bad to go back to the field house, because Jonathan was there, and since he had to behave himself for almost the whole two hours of practice, he had a lot of pent-up screwing around in him, so he'd always think of something stupid to do on the way back to the field house. But once we got changed and set out for the walk home, Jonathan went one way, and I went the other. Since Frankie was gone, I was the only one from my area of town, and it was a long walk. It was longer when it was cold, gray, and drizzling and when the coach had just spent two hours working my butt off and chewing me out. The walk gave me time to think, but there wasn't anything good to think about. When Frankie was around, I'd spend the entire walk home listening to him talk and complain about how he hated the coach, but he always said not to worry because things would get better when the weather improved. But when I was by myself, I had nobody to tell me that I had a chance to win my position and that the coach didn't really think I'd screwed up in practice. When I had to walk home alone and the sky was gray and the hawk was biting, it could get sort of sad. And it was about to get worse.

# CHAPTER 8

# The Wrecker Strikes

By the last week in March, the weather had started to improve. The coach wanted to start getting us ready for some real competition, so he set up an intrasquad game. I got to play shortstop on one team, and my archrival, Darrell, got to play shortstop on the other team. Jonathan was on my team, so we warmed up together. Jonathan didn't figure he'd get a chance to pitch, so he told me he was planning to coach third base. The third-base coach also got to umpire, which appealed to Jonathan. Jonathan asked me if I remembered any of last year's signs, and I said, "No, I don't hardly want to remember any of last year's signs. I'm still trying to learn this year's signs." Then he asked me if I still remembered the steal-nullifier sign, and I just looked back at him as meanly as I could.

Jonathan cracked up and said, "Don't try that stupid white-person scowl on me. You just ain't got what it takes, boy." He went on laughing.

We were the home team, so we took the field first. Since we barely had enough players to make two teams, the coach had to stick some of his excess pitchers out in the outfield, and he stuck Jonathan in right field. Jonathan would coach third base when we were up. I had the normal first-game jitters because I knew I had to make a good impression, or else it would be Scrub City for me. I hoped I'd get my first grounder over with soon because the first was always the hardest.

Sure enough, the leadoff batter, Willie, hit a slow, easy grounder off the bat handle to me. The problem was, Willie happened to be the fastest player on our team, so I charged the ball and, without really thinking, fired an off-balance sidearm throw to first. The throw was perfect, and we got Willie by a half step. I felt great—like a real pro. But then I heard the coach yelling, "Overarm! Overarm! Nice play, kid, but when are you going to learn to throw overarm?" As usual, the coach took me down a notch. I turned my back and kicked the dirt a bit. I knew I'd never really be able to throw overarm, but I figured I'd better try.

I was batting second, which kind of made me feel good, but I knew the only reason I was batting second was because the team was split in half. With the regular squad, I probably would have been either on the bench or batting ninth. I swung real late on a pitch and sliced it down the right-field line. It looked like it was going foul, but I was running as hard as I could anyway, and as I reached first, I saw that it landed just fair and took a wicked hop away from the right fielder, so I raced for second. When

I rounded the bag, I saw Jonathan coaching third and waving me on over. As I approached third, he yelled for me to slide, so I went into one of my patented Yogi Berra headfirst slides. The play was close, but through the big cloud of dust, Jonathan called me safe, which almost caused a rhubarb with the third baseman, who started jumping up and down, saying I was out. Jonathan was relishing his new role as third-base coach and umpire and sure wasn't going to change his mind. If Jonathan the umpire called a base runner out, it would make Jonathan the coach look pretty bad. I was stranded at third as the next two batters made outs.

I made it back to third base in the fourth inning, when I reached first on an error, went to second on a wild pitch, and moved to third on a slow grounder to the first baseman. We were down by only a run thanks to an RBI double by my nemesis, Darrell. I didn't expect the squeeze sign with our number-three hitter, Big Billy, up, so I was kind of surprised when I saw Jonathan tug at his cap and pull his ear, which was the squeeze sign. Or was it? I wasn't sure. Anyway, there was a sign I was supposed to give Jonathan to tell him I'd gotten the original squeeze sign. When I signaled that I had the sign, Jonathan would relay it over to the batter. Well, Jonathan was standing right there next to me, so I just shook my head and whispered, "No." I didn't want to go flying in on a suicide squeeze if I wasn't sure the squeeze sign was really on. Jonathan then flashed a sign to Big Billy. Old Billy laid down the most beautiful bunt ever, and there I was with my feet in cement, still standing at third base. The coach went crazy.

He screamed, "Why the hell didn't you run? Why didn't you run?" I felt like a real jerk, and there was innocent Jonathan, looking out toward center field. The next batter flew out, and when I went back to the bench, the coach chewed me out again.

"A perfect squeeze bunt, and you just stand there. Wake up, will you?"

"But I didn't get the sign," I said.

"If you don't get the sign, you're supposed to ask for time-out."

"But—"

"No buts about it," the coach said, shaking his head in disgust. "Get out there and play."

During the next inning, when we were on the bench, Jonathan wouldn't even look at me. I went over to him and said, "Why'd you give Billy the squeeze sign when I said no?"

"You're supposed to call time-out if you're not sure the squeeze sign has been given. I thought you were just acting to confuse the other team. Don't go trying to get me in trouble when you screw up." Jonathan walked away.

Playing ball just wasn't fun anymore, and it seemed to get less and less fun. By the seventh inning, my team had managed a 3–2 lead, but Darrell led off the top of the seventh with a line-drive single to left. It was his third hit, and each one was a solid line drive. I had managed only my sliced triple in the first inning. Of course, he also threw the ball overarm, and the coach loved that.

One thing Darrell didn't have was speed, so nobody expected it when he took off for second on the first pitch to the next batter. It must have been a hit-and-run play because the batter swung and hit a hot one-hopper to the second baseman. There was one thing I did excel at: taking the throw at second for the double play. I might not have had the greatest arm, but I could get rid of the ball fast, and the relay back to first on the double play was the one time when I could actually get away with throwing the ball sidearm without hearing it from the coach. It was a bang-bang play, the old 4–6–3 double play, and the shortstop had to catch the ball, touch the base, and throw back to first all in one motion. It wasn't the easiest thing in the world because if I wanted to get the batter running to first, I really had to move it, and I couldn't afford to set myself and make the nice, picturesque overarm throw to first that the coach always raved about. In that situation, my sidearm flip worked out well—in practice, of course. There was, however, a bit of a problem in a game with a base runner barreling toward second, ready to bowl me over or slash my ankles with his spikes. That problem got even worse when the guy barreling toward me had gotten a head start because it was a hit-and-run and when the barreling guy was big and reckless, just happened to be fighting for the same position on the team I was, and probably would have loved to slide into me hard enough to break both of my kneecaps. Add to all that a low throw by the second baseman, and I had the makings of a disaster.

I couldn't say if Darrell really wanted to bowl me over or if he just was making a late slide, but I sure didn't intend to do what I did. I was just determined to make that double play and win my job as the starting shortstop. I caught the low throw at my shoe tops and, all in the same motion, touched second base with my foot and fired a sidearm throw toward first. It never got there. The ball hit Darrell right between the eyes as he came sliding in.

The ball made a horrible thud and rolled out into the outfield. My first instinct was to go out after it, but then I realized what I had done. Poor old Darrell was bent over on his knees, moaning away with his hands over his face. I could see blood all over his face and hands. All the other players came running over to see Darrell. When the coach got there, he took charge and yelled for everybody to get out of the way and let Darrell get some air. I felt sick to my stomach and kind of drifted away. Then I heard somebody say, "And the Wrecker strikes again."

Somebody else said sarcastically, "Hey, nice throw, Wrecker."

Then one of Darrell's buddies, a big guy named Calvin, came over and said, "Why'd you go and do that, white boy?"

"Hey, I didn't mean it," I said.

He poked me in the chest. "Why'd you go gunning for my boy, whitey?" Calvin continued to taunt me. "You're gonna pay for this."

Just then, Jonathan came along and said, "Hey, Calvin, lay off, will ya? The guy didn't mean it."

"Yeah, well, man, the friggin' guy hit my man Darrell right in the head."

"Hey, man, the guy didn't mean it. That's why they call him the Wrecker, man," Jonathan said.

Soon the ambulance arrived, and the ambulance squad carefully placed Darrell on a stretcher. A few other guys came over to me and started razzing me.

"Nice going, Wrecker. That's one way to get a starting spot. Eliminate the competition."

Then the coach announced that practice was over. He went with Darrell in the ambulance, and they drove off to the hospital. Everybody headed back to the field house. Big Billy came up to me.

"Even if you was as big as me, I wouldn't want to be you when Darrell gets better. He's a mean one," Big Billy said.

"Thanks," I said, and Big Billy walked on ahead. I was the last one to leave the field, and I felt terrible. What a jerk I was. I'd hit the guy right in the head. Just then, Jonathan popped up out of nowhere.

"I figured I'd better wait around and walk you back to the field house," he said. "It's dangerous out here for you after what you did today. Word spreads fast."

"Thanks a lot, Jonathan. Thanks for the encouragement," I said.

"Hey, look. Don't worry about it. Darrell will be fine. His head is harder than any ole baseball anyway," Jonathan said, and for the first time since the accident had happened, I began to feel a little better.

"Seriously, I wouldn't worry about Darrell if I were you," he added. "He'll probably be okay. But I would worry about *you* if I were you. You know these black kids from Roosevelt School have a bit of a different way of dealing with things than we integrated folks. And they don't hardly like it when one of their boys is flattened with a baseball between the eyes, especially from someone with such an obvious motive like you."

"But I didn't mean to do it, Jonathan," I said.

"I know. But you may have trouble convincing some of Darrell's buddies," Jonathan said.

He was right about that.

CHAPTER 9

# Somebody Always Gets the Good Ones

Our first game was on Tuesday, April 2, and I was the starting shortstop. Darrell was out of the hospital and walking around, but his face looked awful. He had stitches across his forehead, his left eye was black and blue and swollen, and there was no telling when he'd be able to play again. He was at the game, in the bleachers, wearing his normal school clothes. I still felt bad about the whole thing, and other than Jonathan and maybe Big Billy, it didn't seem like anybody on the team wanted to talk to me. I wanted to apologize to Darrell, but I was kind of scared to. Darrell always hung around with Calvin and his buddies, and I felt like they wanted to get even with me. Jonathan was kind of supportive of me, but I could see he was in danger of losing the respect of the black kids if he hung around me too much. Jonathan never admitted it, but I could see that he always had to balance out things with his white friends and his black friends, especially on the baseball team.

Jonathan hung around with a lot of us white kids, and he did it rather naturally. His neighborhood was integrated, and so was the grammar school he'd gone to, so he got along pretty well with white kids. Of course, since he was in the advanced class and most of us were white, he kind of had to get along with us. However, he knew just the same that if he hung around with only white kids, the other black kids would be pissed off at him.

I once heard Darrell refer to Jonathan as a honky lover, which was an image that Jonathan tried to avoid. On our JV squad, Jonathan and I were the only kids in the advanced classes, and most of the black kids were from Roosevelt School and didn't normally have much to do with the white kids, so Jonathan had to walk a fine line on the team. I thought I was his best friend on the team, and he was mine, but Jonathan had to be careful not to let the Roosevelt School kids know that, because he didn't want to have the image of a honky lover. The disaster with Darrell had made things even worse. Battling Darrell for the shortstop job had been tough since I knew that most of the Roosevelt School kids were rooting for Darrell. Even if I'd beat out Darrell fair and square, there would have been resentment, but now that I'd put Darrell out of the competition physically, there was more than just resentment; there was downright hatred. Jonathan was caught right in the middle.

Jonathan wanted to try to help me along because he could see I was in pretty bad shape and in need of a friend, but he knew that now it was even worse for him to be seen hanging out with a white kid, especially when that white kid happened to be me. But if anybody could handle such a situation, it was Jonathan. He'd once said that a black person could only be president if he knew how to get along with the white folks without having his black brothers and sisters hate him. He said that Dr. Martin Luther King Jr. was still trying to figure out a way to get along with white folks, but by the time Jonathan was ready to run for president, he said getting along with white folks would be easy. Still getting along with black folks would be the hard part. But above all, Jonathan would say, "You've got to make sure your upper lip doesn't sweat like it did for Richard Nixon during his televised debate with JFK." He said that was what had lost Nixon the election in 1960, and Jonathan said old Richard Nixon still didn't have a chance in '68 because his upper lip was still sweating.

Jonathan would walk with me down to Roosevelt Field. We would talk about stuff that went on in our classes, and he would kind of act as my bodyguard, but when we got to the field, he'd warm up with Calvin. I would warm up with Big Billy because I could see he felt a little sorry for me. But I could also see that in a way, some of the white kids were kind of happy I'd beaned Darrell. Darrell wasn't much of a favorite with anybody except his Roosevelt School buddies, and even some of them were friendly to Darrell more out of fear than because they liked him. Most of the white kids downright hated ole

Darrell. A couple of them actually came up to me and thanked me for doing what they'd been wanting to do all along. I didn't know what to say to that. It was nice to be looked at as a hero, even though it wasn't true, but I sure would need some help if any of Darrell's friends tried to get even. In a way, it made me uncomfortable because some of those white guys disliked Darrell not because he was obnoxious but because he was black. Some of them didn't like Jonathan for the same reason. The only one who was strictly nonpartial was the coach. I knew he was upset about losing Darrell because he'd been leaning toward Darrell as his starting shortstop. But Darrell could be just as much of a pain to the coach as he could to anybody else, so maybe he didn't mind having Darrell out of trouble, sitting in the stands.

There was one thing the coach did care about, and I thought it was probably the only thing he cared about: winning. To him, winning was everything. Now that I was his starting shortstop, he was on my back even more. It didn't go beyond his expert observation that the reason my throw hit Darrell in the face in the first place was because I threw the ball sidearm. If there was ever anybody who relished the opportunity to say, "I told you so," it was the coach. He didn't even mention the fact that I nearly had decapitated his probable starting shortstop. All he could say was "With a good overarm throw, you would have gotten the double play."

I was batting seventh in the order, and of course, I was not allowed to switch-hit. A big right-hander was pitching for Hillsdale, and he had a big, slow curveball I knew would drive me crazy while batting right-handed. Among my many shortcomings as a ballplayer was my inability to hit a curveball. Pitchers at the JV level didn't have curveballs like old Sandy Koufax's, but still, with just the slightest break, I didn't have a chance. I did better when switch-hitting because I could hit a curveball better when batting lefty, but the coach was the coach, and if I wanted to play at all, I had to play the way he said.

I struck out my first two times up. The first time, the pitcher threw me a pitch that I swore was heading right for my head, so I ducked, and the umpire called it strike three. The next time, I was determined to swing, so I struck out swinging at a pitch in the dirt.

The score was tied going into the bottom of the sixth. We had managed only two hits, but one of them was a three-run homer by Big Billy. We were pretty lucky to be holding Hillsdale to only three runs, thanks basically to their lousy hitting and some good defense by the outfield. Some credit also went to our pitcher, Meatball Joe, who seemed to have improved quite a bit since last year, when he'd earned his nickname Meatball because of all the meatballs he'd dished out to the opposing batters, which they'd usually deposited somewhere in the trees out behind left-center field. Meatball Joe always prided himself on his good control, which he was right about. He rarely walked anybody—but that was because he always dished out such delicious meatballs that batters rarely even took a pitch. In fact, they usually didn't even foul a ball off. They just got up there and swung. It was nice out in the field. The outfielders never had to wait around like they did with other pitchers who had no control. Meatball Joe was always around the plate, and the coach made sure his outfielders were playing deep. Although Meatball had let up ten hits in six innings, he allowed no walks and only three runs.

Since most of the action was in the outfield, I had a very easy day at short. I handled two grounders with no problem and caught one liner that was hit so hard it almost broke through my webbing. I led off the bottom of the sixth, and I was determined not to swing at a bad ball. The Hillsdale pitcher was getting a little wild, so I decided to take a few pitches. Four was all I needed because he missed with every one, and I had a walk. The next batter laid down a perfect sacrifice, and I made it to second. The coach sent up a pinch hitter for Meatball Joe, a guy named Gorski, who could hit like crazy but couldn't field a lick. The first pitch to him was wild and skipped by the catcher, so I took off for third. The ball must have bounced right off the backstop to the catcher because there was a close play at third. I could hear Jonathan, the third-base coach, yell, "Slide!" so I went into my patented Yogi Berra headfirst slide.

There was a cloud of dust, and my hat went flying, and then I heard the umpire yell, "Safe!" Jonathan later claimed I was out, but he made the safe sign just the same in order to sway the umpire, who was umpiring from behind home plate and therefore, because of the distance and all the dust, could hardly see anything. Most of the other players agreed with Jonathan, but they said the only reason Jonathan made the safe sign was because he thought he was still umpiring in an intrasquad game. Gorski then promptly hit the next pitch for a double, and I scored. Gorski eventually came around to score on another hit, and we had a two-run lead going into the top of the seventh.

The coach sent in his new pitcher, a black kid with the last name of Puddle. His first name was Arthur, but everybody called him Mud. Well, ole Mud didn't exactly have his good stuff and was dishing up pitches tastier than Meatball's. He faced four batters, letting in one run and managing to get one out, before the coach yanked him and brought in Jonathan. The score was 5–4 with one out and runners on second and third. As Jonathan warmed up, I could see he had his Bob Gibson fastball, but I could also see he had no control. The coach probably figured that with first base open, Jonathan would have a little breathing room, and because Jonathan happened to be his only other relief pitcher, it was either him or Puddle. Jonathan promptly lost his breathing room with his first pitch—his patented Bob Gibson brush-back pitch— which hit his first batter right in the back. The bases were loaded, and it was getting a bit tense out there. I prayed the next batter wouldn't hit anything my way, but I knew that with Jonathan pitching, the batter was more likely to get hit than hit the ball.

The second batter Jonathan faced was Hillsdale's number-three hitter, a guy who had been blasting the ball all over the field against Meatball Joe. Jonathan had one thing in his favor: the Hillsdale batters were used to digging in with Meatball Joe's fat pitches. They could kind of lean over the plate and get a good look at Meatball's control pitches. Well, Jonathan didn't have any control pitches, as his first batter found out. It wasn't smart to dig in and crowd the plate with Jonathan on the mound unless one was wearing a suit of armor. That was the mistake the number-three hitter on Hillsdale's team made against Jonathan. He was digging in real good and real aggressively, ready to clobber whatever Jonathan could dish out. Well, Jonathan let go one of his all-time-best Bob Gibson brush-back pitches, and it headed right for the head of the Hillsdale batter. As the guy went sprawling to get out of the way of the pitch, he put his bat up in front of his head for protection. Well, the ball hit his bat, which sent a nice little one-hopper right back to Jonathan. Jonathan caught the ball and carefully flipped it underhand to the catcher, who stepped on the plate for the force on the runner coming from third and then calmly tagged the Hillside number-three batter, who was still sprawled in the batter's box. *Double play!* We won! We all went out to mob Jonathan as if it were the final game of the World Series. All the while, most of us were laughing our heads off. Jonathan tried to act cool about it, but we could see that he was laughing too, even though he claimed that was the way he had planned it all along.

Our euphoria didn't last long. We lost our next game on Thursday, 9–1. I managed one hit in three at bats but made two errors. We were pretty subdued in the field house. Jonathan hadn't played, so he didn't shower. I was slowly undressing at my locker, feeling kind of depressed, and Jonathan came up behind me and tapped me on the shoulder. I turned around, and he had on one of those ridiculous Groucho Marx eyeglass disguises. He gave a big smile and held out a pencil as if it were a cigar. Seeing that big black face with that stupid Groucho Marx mask and that stupid smile, I couldn't help but burst out laughing. However, as I started laughing, everybody turned around to look, and Jonathan quickly took off the mask, stuffed it into his athletic bag, switched his demented smile to a somber frown, and headed toward the field house door. In the background, I heard the coach grumble, "I didn't think there'd be anything to laugh about when you lose nine to one."

I decided not to shower and just got the heck out of there. When I got home, I went right upstairs. My mother yelled up, "Did ya win?"

"No," I said.

"Well, your supper's on the stove," she said.

"Yeah, yeah. I'll be right down," I said, but I was in a bad mood and in no rush to eat. I turned on the radio for some music, but there was some special news report. Martin Luther King Jr. had been shot. *Oh my God.* I couldn't believe it. I felt sick to my stomach. I rushed downstairs to the living room, and my father was sitting there, watching the news on TV.

"Is it true?" I asked. "Somebody shot Martin Luther King?"

"Yeah, they got 'im," my father said. "Somebody always gets the good ones."

I didn't know whether or not my father liked the Doc or even cared a hoot about him, but I could see that my father was really upset. "Yep. They got 'im. He did good for his people." My father was shaking his head. "He was a good one, but they got 'im." My father got really cynical sometimes when he got upset, and I could see he was getting cynical.

"Is it real bad?" I asked.

"Looks that way," he said.

*Oh my God*, I thought. *What about Jonathan?* I quickly went into the bedroom to phone Jonathan. His line was busy. I tried again after a minute, and Lendora answered. I asked her if she'd heard the news, and she said of course she'd heard the news. She said her house was crazy. Her father had gone into a rage, swearing and cursing, and now he was at the kitchen table, just sobbing. She said her mother was praying nonstop. Lendora said she wished they'd stop with all the stupid news reports so she could watch some decent television shows. I asked her about Jonathan, and she said he was up in his room with the door locked. I asked if I could talk to him, but she said she didn't think I should. Then Lendora asked me if I had heard that a white person had done the shooting. I said I hadn't known that. She said she'd heard Jonathan say that it was a white man just as he was locking himself in the room upstairs.

When I hung up, I headed right upstairs, but my mother intercepted me to remind me that my supper was getting cold. I said I didn't feel good and just wanted to be left alone.

"You really should eat," she said, but I just bolted upstairs and closed the door. A little while later, a news report came through. Dr. Martin Luther King Jr. was dead.

There was trouble at school the next day. I could feel the tension in the halls. I desperately wanted to talk to Jonathan, but he had stayed home. For the most part the black kids and white kids had always gotten along okay at our school. But occasionally there were some problems. There were fights here and there and arguments sometimes—but nothing like what happened that day. I didn't know how it started, but it was a lousy, ugly mess.

As we were changing classes for the second period, I headed toward the main hallway on my way up to history class. I heard some screams and then some rumbling coming from the second floor. The hallway was pretty crowded, and all of a sudden, I saw a kid running down the stairs into the main hallway. He wasn't saying anything, but everybody started screaming; his face was covered with blood. I'd never seen anything like it. I didn't know who he was, but he was staggering and looked awful. Then I heard more scuffling and screaming, and two other kids came running down the stairs, screaming, "They're gonna kill us!" Everybody was sort of milling around because we didn't know what to do, but we could still hear yelling, rumbling, and fighting coming from the second floor. Just then, I saw Frankie tearing down the hall. He was yelling, "They've got the whole class trapped in there!"

"Where?" I asked. Suddenly, a whole bunch of girls came screaming down the stairs.

"They must have let the girls go," Frankie said.

"Who?" I asked.

"I'm not sure," Frankie said. "It's bunch of black kids who said they're looking for somebody."

"Who?" I asked.

"Beats me," Frankie said. "But it's scary up there."

Just then, another kid came tearing down the stairs. He was all bloodied too, and he was yelling, "Fire! Fire! They started a fire!" We then saw smoke drifting down the stairs. More kids ran down the stairs, and they were coughing and wiping their eyes. By that time, there was mass confusion in the main hall. Everybody started screaming and yelling and heading for the main doors. Some teachers finally came out and tried to calm everybody down. Maybe they wanted a chance to practice a real-life fire drill, but it sure wasn't working out the way it did all the times we practiced without any real fire. Finally, the cops arrived. They were going to head upstairs, but they quickly saw that the fire department was needed, so the cops just took over for the hysterical teachers, who were hardly doing any good with the fire drill. The cops quickly booted everybody out.

Soon the fire trucks arrived, but they pulled up in the parking lot in back of the school, so all of us in the front went around to the back of the school to check it out. I stuck with Frankie, and when we got to the back of the school, we could see smoke pouring out of Mr. Hackney's biology classroom. By then, the firemen had hooked up their hoses, and they were shooting water up at the second floor. It didn't take long to put the fire out, and the firemen went upstairs to assess the damage. There was quite a bit, and they came down with a rather badly damaged Mr. Hackney, who was covered with soot and didn't look like he was breathing. An ambulance pulled up and carted Mr. Hackney away with a few other kids who were coughing, gagging, and bleeding. Mr. Krauzer then arrived on the scene, and after conferring with the fire chief, he told everybody to go home.

"That's a switch," Frankie said. "Hey, that's great! Mr. Krauzer is actually telling us to go home early! All right! No school! Let's get out of here. Almost a whole day off!"

Just then, one of Frankie's friends came over, a guy named Ronnie. "Hey, Frankie boy," Ronnie said. "We and the boys kinda figure we'd better try to figure out what we are gonna do about these coloreds. Ya know? We gotta protect ourselves. Dig?"

"Yeah. You're right," Frankie said.

"What do ya say, T. J.?" Ronnie asked.

"Ah. No. Ah. Not really," I said. "You know who started it?"

"Yeah. Some coloreds started it," Ronnie snarled. "We gotta fight back. Dig?" Ronnie had long, slicked-back black hair. He was what most of us called a hood.

"Yeah," I said, but I wasn't really convinced about who'd started the fire or the fighting.

"Well, come on. Let's go," Ronnie said.

"Yeah. Okay," Frankie said. "Come on, T. J. We gotta protect ourselves."

Well, there was no way I wanted to start hanging out with Ronnie and his boys, but I didn't know how to say no. "Yeah. Well, look. I, ah, want to go check on ole Mr.

Hackney now. And then maybe I'll check you guys out. Okay?"

"Mr. Hackney—suckface! Who the heck cares about him?" Ronnie sneered. "Ah. Come on, Frankie boy."

The next thing Ronnie said really floored me: "Ah. He's a colored lover anyway."

Then they both left. Frankie kind of had a guilty look, but he went off with Ronnie. I hadn't realized I had an image as a colored lover—whatever that was. I guessed it was the flip side of the honky-lover image Jonathan tried to avoid. Maybe Ronnie was right. But who cared? All I really wanted to do was see Jonathan and tell him how sorry I was and how bad I felt about the Doc. I wanted to tell him that the guy who'd shot the Doc was probably just a lunatic. But Jonathan wasn't around. The only things around were a lot of leftover smoke, dripping water, and a lot of hate.

There was more trouble that night. Frankie told me all about it the next day. I sat at home and watched *Star Trek*. I wasn't interested in it much and went to bed early, listening to the radio. Frankie told me he was out cruising with Ronnie and some of the boys. He said they had chains and bats in the car for protection. They were out looking for revenge. The kids who'd been bloodied in the fight at school were some of Ronnie's buddies, and Ronnie swore to get even. Well, Frankie said that a fight broke out at the downtown pizza parlor between Ronnie's boys and some black kids. The police were out in numbers and broke up the fight.

Then there was another fire over in the black section of town, followed by an incident in which a gang of black kids invaded the white Jefferson School area, threw rocks, and broke a bunch of windows at the school. Frankie told me there were three or four fires on Elm Street, and there were cops and fire trucks everywhere. Frankie said that all in all, it was a pretty darn exciting night. He told me that the police had put on a 9:00 p.m. curfew and that his mother was going to lock him in the house at night. The two kids who'd gotten bloodied at school were sent to the hospital to be stitched up because they had pretty bad cuts from being hit in the head with a broomstick. They were okay, though. He said they looked a lot worse than they really were because of all the blood dripping over their faces. Frankie said that Mr. Hackney was all right. He'd just suffered some smoke inhalation. Some of the other kids had suffered smoke inhalation, but they were okay too. Frankie said the fight had started because some of the black kids were pissed off about Martin Luther King Jr. being shot, and Ronnie's friend made a stupid comment about how King was better off dead. Then Frankie said there was a rumor about Darrell's friends using the King assassination as an excuse to go after one of Darrell's enemies. Frankie paused when he reached that part of the story.

"They think Darrell's friends may be seeking revenge against the guy who beaned Darrell with a baseball."

"Oh great," I said.

"But don't worry," Frankie said. "Right now, I think the black kids are ready to beat up anybody's who's white.

And of course, the white kids want to beat up anybody who's black. So don't worry. Everybody's after everybody."

That wasn't very reassuring. Then Frankie told me that school was on for Monday, but there might be cops in the hallways. There would be no extracurricular activities until further notice, including JV baseball.

"I guess that's for your protection, huh?" Frankie laughed.

"Great joke," I said sarcastically.

Then Frankie got serious. "Oh. And about what Ronnie said yesterday about you being a colored lover? Yeah, well, I know that Ronnie's basically a creep and all, but he and a lot of his friends don't like black kids. You know? And after all this stuff, I think they really hate black kids. You know? And they know that you are really good friends with Jonathan and all. And well, you know, it kind of looks bad."

I could feel my blood start to boil. "What looks bad? What?"

"Hey, well, look. You know, I don't care. Hey, I think Jonathan's a pretty good guy myself. And hey, look. He even rescued me from the subways and all. And you know I like some black kids. But look. Some of these white kids are really pissed off, you know? They see all this rioting and stuff on TV. And they see these black guys stealing stuff and burning stuff—and then with this stuff right in our own town. Wow! There's a lot of totally pissed-off people."

"And also a lot of people with nothing else to do but cruise the streets and look for trouble," I said.

"True," Frankie said. "But hey, look. Just for your own protection, maybe you shouldn't hang around with Jonathan for a while."

"Yeah, don't worry. Jonathan doesn't want to hang around with me anyway," I said. "He's really broken up about the Doc getting murdered, and he probably is blaming all white people, including me, for it."

"Yeah, well, look. I'm just trying to help ya out, you know? We're still buddies, you know?"

"Yeah. Yeah, Frankie," I said with disgust.

There were a few more fires on Saturday night, but they weren't nearly as bad as the ones the night before. I phoned Jonathan again but talked to Lendora, who said Jonathan still didn't want to talk to me. School was back in session on Monday, and it seemed there were more cops than students. A lot of the kids stayed home, including Jonathan, who I was sure wasn't scared but still depressed. They called off school on Tuesday because it was the day of Martin Luther King Jr.'s funeral, or maybe they called off school because nobody was coming anyway. I watched most of the funeral stuff on TV. It was mostly pretty boring, but they showed some stuff about the Doc's career—stuff I didn't even know about. They showed some films of his speeches. I especially liked the one about his dream and all that stuff—with black and white kids going to school together and being friends. But it sure seemed like nothing more than a dream.

One report focused on all the riots since the Doc was shot. Something like forty people had died. The report even mentioned our town. It was the first time I ever had seen anything about our town on stupid television. It wasn't complimentary when they described the town as a "racially torn town that has experienced several disturbances and even a fire in its school." I was thankful they didn't mention my sidearm throw that had beaned Darrell. Later on, they showed shots of the thousands of people at the funeral. They showed all the celebrities who were there, including Wilt "the Stilt" Chamberlain, Jackie Kennedy, Bobby Kennedy, and even ole Richard Nixon. Sure enough, if I looked close, I could see that Nixon's upper lip was sweaty. I wondered if Jonathan had noticed it.

# CHAPTER 10

# Lendora to
# the Rescue

The next day, school was back in session. Jonathan was back, and cops were all over the place. There had been another incident of what the stupid newspapers were calling racial strife, but it actually had just been Ronnie and his boys cruising through the black section, looking for revenge. Frankie said they'd beat up some black kids, but that was all—no fires or anything. I thought Frankie was a little disappointed. Since Mr. Hackney's biology class was all burned out, biology class was in the lunchroom. We got to sit wherever we wanted, and it seemed Jonathan tried his best to sit as far away from me as possible. He sat next to one of the other two black kids, and he was real quiet throughout the entire class, which was incredible considering old Mr. Hackney was out recovering from his ordeal and we had a real dippy substitute. Jonathan relished substitutes. He could wrap them around his finger, and with all the whites so afraid of blacks, Jonathan could have had a ball with this substitute. But he was silent for the whole class. It was a boring class. Most of the kids were just waiting for Jonathan to start some kind of screwing around. When he didn't, the class dragged along and seemed to last for hours.

I guessed it was tough when something terrible happened to your hero. I was sure I'd go crazy if something happened to the Mick. But I guessed it was a lot worse when something terrible happened to somebody millions of people loved. The Doc was the hero of a lot more people than just a bunch of dopey kids or baseball fans. It was kind of like when John F. Kennedy was assassinated. I was just a little squirt at the time, but just about the whole country was shocked and upset. My mother was crying away, and it was the first time I could ever remember my father walking around shaking his head. The networks had lots of news stories when President Kennedy was shot—lots of boring stuff, but they showed films of JFK playing with his kids and all, and there was a shot of the little squirt John John saluting his father's casket. It was all real sad. We got a few days off from school, and I was pretty darn happy about that. Some of the films about JFK showed Bobby Kennedy too. I'd always thought Bobby was a lot cooler than his brother—maybe because I was partial to younger brothers. Jonathan said that his family were big JFK supporters, and they were very upset when JFK was assassinated, but I was sure this was a lot worse.

I knew firsthand how Jonathan worshipped the Doc, and his folks did too. I knew this had to be real hard on them. But I couldn't understand why Jonathan wouldn't speak to me. He wouldn't even look at me. I mean, what the heck were friends for anyway? You were supposed to be able to share your grief and all that stuff, and anyway, I liked the Doc too. Maybe some people thought that because I was white, I shouldn't have cared or something. Or maybe Jonathan blamed me because I was white. Maybe he thought all white people were to blame.

Biology class was as boring as ever, and every time I looked over at Jonathan, he was either looking down at his biology book or staring out the window.

The ban on after-school activities had been lifted, so our game that afternoon at Roosevelt Field was on. Nobody seemed psyched about playing it. Most of the white kids were apprehensive about going to Roosevelt Field. Jonathan stayed as far away from me as he could, so I stayed near most of the other white guys. When we got to the field, I warmed up with Big Billy. When we were done throwing, Big Billy took me aside and said, "You stick with us, kiddo. We heard some of them coloreds are out to get you. We're gonna keep our eyes on you. Come here, and look at this." Big Billy took off his cap and showed me that he had a razor blade in the lining. "No Roosevelt School colored is gonna mess with me."

"Yeah. Yeah, that's great, Big Billy," I said, and I went over to the bat rack to check for my bat and to get away from him.

The game started off pretty raggedly, as if both teams were out of practice. I made a throwing error in the first inning—what else was new?—but I made a good play on a line drive in the second to rob a hit. Darrell, bandages and all, and some of his buddies were over in the stands, and I started to get a bit worried. I didn't feel any better when Big Billy came over and tried again to reassure me. "Darrell's buddies are here, but don't worry. I heard that Ronnie and some of his boys are going to cruise over here to make sure everything is all right."

*I'll bet*, I thought. They'd just be out there looking for trouble, I figured.

In the fourth inning, I got a hanging curve and drilled it down the left-field line for a double. It was my best hit of the year, and to be honest, I was pretty darn surprised I could hit a ball that well. I was a heck of a lot more surprised when I heard somebody from the stands cheer, "Atta boy, T. J.!" I looked over and could hardly believe it: in the bleachers was Jonathan's dumb little sister Lendora. She was there with one of her other little girlfriends, and I had to admit it made me feel good to have a few fans rooting for me. I was sure Darrell and his buddies were hoping I would drop dead. I came around to score on a hit by Gorski, and the game was tied 3–3. Lendora let out another cheer as I crossed the plate. I wondered what my various adversaries were thinking when they saw a little black kid cheering for me. Racial strife could really complicate things.

Unfortunately, that hit was the last thing my fans had to cheer about. The other team went on to score four runs and build up a 7–3 lead, but then we started to rally in the bottom of the seventh. I was due up fifth in the inning, and I worried about making the last out of the game. I was one for three, but the only time I'd hit the ball hard was on my double. I wasn't exactly a picture of confidence at the plate. So even though I was kind of rooting for the team to get a rally going, deep down, I was just hoping I wouldn't have to get up with two out. It was the worst feeling in the world for a player to make the last out in a game. I hated it.

Well, sure enough, we got a rally going. The first guy walked. Then there was an error and then a base hit. One run scored, and Pitman, the guy before me, was up with first and second, no outs, and a score of 7–4. We were getting excited on the bench, but then ole Pitman popped out for the first out. When I got up, I was as nervous as heck. I heard Lendora cheering for me, but that made me even more nervous. Sometimes it was better not to have any fans around so there was nobody around to see you when you screwed up. I was hoping for another hanging curve because this guy knew curveballs were my weakness. Sure enough, the first pitch was a big, fat curveball hanging right out there where I liked it, so I swung as hard as I could—and missed the pitch by a mile. It curved. The next pitch was the same thing, but it didn't curve, and I hit a hot smash down the third-base line. Unfortunately, the third baseman made a backhanded stab just like old Clete Boyer of the Yanks. Then he stepped on third base for the force out and fired across the diamond, where I was hardly even halfway to first. *Double play! Unbelievable.* I had made not only the last out but the last two outs—Depression City. I felt awful as I walked slowly back to the bench, and everybody started packing up. I sat down alone on the end. I heard Lendora say from over in the bleachers, "Nice wood anyway, T. J." I looked over, and she and her little girlfriend were heading out toward the street. She gave a little goodbye wave.

As I was sitting there by myself, Big Billy came by. I thought he was going to offer me some words of consolation, but instead, he told me I'd better get going because Darrell and his boys were still waiting around, and Big Billy didn't think it would be safe for me to leave Roosevelt Field alone. I was still upset about the game, and I got pissed off about what Big Billy was saying.

"Hey, look, Billy," I said. "Don't you think you're carrying this thing a little too far? Christ sakes. There ain't nobody after me."

"Yeah?" Big Billy said. "Well, look, buddy boy. I'm only trying to help you. You know we got to take care of our own."

"What do you mean 'our own'?" I asked. "White kids got to take care of white kids because all the blacks are out to get us?"

"Yeah, that's exactly what I mean," Big Billy said. He was starting to get mad.

"Well, look, Billy. I can darn well take care of myself without you and your buddies looking after me and trying to stir up trouble."

"Stir up trouble? What the heck are you talking about? The coloreds are the ones stirring up the trouble."

"Oh, come on, Billy," I said. "I heard about Ronnie and his boys beating up an innocent black kid just last night." I was really getting pissed.

"Innocent? Who cares if the kid was innocent? He was a colored, wasn't he? Ronnie just wants revenge," Big Billy said.

"Yeah, revenge," I said sarcastically.

"So what's with you, T. J., anyway? Why are you always defending these coloreds?" Big Billy was starting to get pretty darn mad now.

"Yeah, well, look," I said. "I know why that fight started in school. It started because somebody was cursing out the Doc." I didn't mean to say *the Doc*, but it slipped out.

"The Doc? Who the hell is the Doc?" Big Billy didn't know what I meant, and I was glad. "The fight started, buddy boy, because Darrell and his boys wanted to get even with you for just about knocking Darrell's block off with a baseball, something that a lot of us white kids would love to have the opportunity to do. And if you'll just lookee yonder, you'll see Darrell's boys still hanging around like a bunch of vultures, just waiting to get a crack at you."

"You're crazy, Billy!" I was really upset. I got up and headed out toward the outfield to head back to the field house. I did not want to believe what Big Billy was saying. I was still not sure if it was true, and I sure didn't want to believe it.

"Well, suit yourself, buddy," Big Billy said. "Oh, and good luck. You'll need it."

As I headed away from Big Billy, I headed out the way Jonathan used to show me. It was a shortcut that Jonathan and I would use in order to get back to the field house first. Jonathan never liked to waste any time, especially his free time. I thought it was the best way to get away from Big Billy and any of his friends, and sure enough, I was right, but there was one problem: the shortcut went right through one of the poor sections of the black neighborhood. I realized that might be the neighborhood Darrell lived in. I quickened my pace. I had never been afraid to go through that section, but that had been before the fights at school, and I'd been with Jonathan. There were quite a few people walking around. It was a nice spring afternoon. A few flowers were popping up. I didn't know what kinds they were except for the dandelions, which didn't really qualify as flowers. There were plenty of dandelions. The sidewalks were cracked and crumbled, so I was walking in the street. There were plenty of parked cars around on the street, and some of them looked sort of beat up. I hardly thought someone could actually drive them. Every time people walked past me, I tried not to look at them, but I knew they were looking at me. They were probably thinking, *What the heck is this white kid doing, walking through here all by himself? Is he crazy or something?* I guessed I must have been.

A bunch of little kids were playing kickball or something in the street. I didn't want to get them upset or anything, so I waited a bit for an opportunity to go by unnoticed, but that was pretty hard with a bunch of dopey kids. Even though they were a lot younger than I was, that didn't stop them from taunting me. "Hey, white boy. What choo doin' round here?" one little kid said. I tried to act cool and ignored him.

"Yeah, white boy. Go on back to yo' own neighborhood," a little girl said. She was even younger than Lendora.

I decided I'd go up onto the curb and walk around them, but there was no sidewalk; there was just somebody's lawn, so I figured I'd have to cut through their game. Just then, I heard some kids coming down the street behind me. I could tell they were kind of rowdy. It sounded like a gang. I turned around and saw Darrell and his buddies. I knew I was in big trouble. As I looked back, I could see that they noticed me. I was a sitting duck.

"Hey, man, look who's here," I heard Darrell say. "This white boy wants to see how the other half lives."

"Hey, man, it's the Wrecker. What a treat," another kid said. "Let's show him round the 'hood."

I started walking faster, and I walked right into a little kid.

"Hey, get out of here, man," the little kid said.

"Yeah. Ah. Sure," I said. "I'm sorry." I sure was sorry—about a lot of things. I was sorry I'd come this way, sorry I'd ignored Big Billy, sorry the Doc had gotten blown away, and darn sorry that I threw sidearm.

"Hey, what you messing up the kids' game for?" Darrell said.

"Ah, I'm just heading back to the field house," I said. I was walking backward while talking to Darrell, who was still several yards away from me. I had gotten beyond the kids' game, but I was still deep in the heart of Darrell's neighborhood.

"Um, uh, how's the ole eye?" I managed to say, and then I regretted saying it.

"It's still pretty messed up," one of Darrell's buddies said. "How 'bout if we make your eye just like his—and maybe both of them."

"Yeah," another kid said. They started to move toward me more quickly. I was still walking backward. I knew that if I turned my back to them, I'd better run, but I didn't think I could outrun them all. As they got closer, however, I thought my only escape would be to run. I still had the speed of a young Mickey Mantle, or so I liked to think, but I was so scared that I couldn't get up the nerve to turn around and run. Just then, a car horn honked. The car drove through the kickball game and then went through Darrell's gang. I was kind of hoping it was a police car or something, but I had no such luck. As it drove by me, I saw that a bunch of black people were inside.

Suddenly, just as the car was passing me, it jerked to a stop, and I heard somebody call my name. "Hey, T. J.! What you doin' over here? How 'bout a ride?" It was Lendora—good ole lovely, wonderful, little, dopey Lendora and her stupid wonderful friends being driven home by one of their fathers.

I went up to the car slowly. I gulped a little, tried to maintain my cool, and said, "Ah. Yeah. Sure. Why not?" I hopped in, and we were off.

"What you doin' walking through this section of town, T. J.?" Lendora said as we drove back toward the field house.

"Ah, it's a shortcut," I managed to say. "Jonathan taught me it."

"Oh," Lendora said thoughtfully. "You know, T. J., white boys shouldn't be walkin' through this section of town alone these days. And ooh boy, you do look white! You seen a ghost?" Lendora sure could be very perceptive sometimes.

They let me off back at the field house. No way was I going to take a shower. I changed and was out of the place in a blink. I did still have that young Mickey Mantle speed, I thought, because I got home in record time, running all the way.

# CHAPTER 11

# That Mr. Tambourine Man Fellow

As bad as things were at school and on the baseball team, things got even worse when my brother came home from college on spring break. It was his first year at college, and in a way, I kind of missed him. However, things were a lot different now that we were older, and when he got back on spring break, boy, were things different. Somebody said my brother had become a hippie or something, but all I knew was that when he got home, he did nothing but argue with my parents. Just about every single night for the entire week, my brother would start arguing with my parents about something. First, it was his hair. I didn't think he'd had it cut since he went away. I thought it looked really neat, but my mother was pretty darn pissed off.

"When are you going to cut your hair?" she'd ask.

"When hell freezes over," he'd reply.

Then she'd say something real dumb, like "You're not going to church with your hair like that."

Then my brother would say something like "Good. I didn't plan on going to church anyway." Of course, that would get my mother even madder and more upset.

Then my brother would start playing his rock albums on the living room stereo. He'd play some Beatles albums, and he had an album by some guys called Cream—my mother couldn't stand it. My brother would play the song "Sunshine of Your Love" over and over again, and it would drive my mother nuts. Usually, the only kinds of records that ever got played on our stereo were things like Tony Bennett and Perry Como. I guessed the Cream album was pretty much of a shock to my mother *and* our stereo. I felt a little sorry for my mother because my brother didn't seem to care much about what she said. My brother never used to be like that. As a matter of fact, my brother always was kind of a model student, a model son, and even a model brother. Well, he sure wasn't much of a model anything anymore.

The album my parents really couldn't stand was by a guy my parents said couldn't sing a lick. The guy's name was Bob Dylan, and the album was a bunch of his greatest hits. I didn't know what was so great about them since the only one I'd ever heard of was a song called "Blowin' in the Wind," and Peter, Paul, and Mary sure sang it a lot better than he did. My father once had to order my brother to take that album off the stereo. "Get that off right now!" he said. I hardly ever saw my father get that mad. I hadn't heard him raise his voice like that since we were real little squirts. I didn't think the album was good either, and the guy did have a weird voice, but there was one song about a Mr. Tambourine Man guy that I thought was sort of neat. I listened to the song a few times when nobody was around. I liked it. I kind of wished I knew somebody like that Mr. Tambourine Man fellow.

The worst arguments of all were about the stupid war in Vietnam.

"We'd better get out of there," my brother'd say. "That idiot President Johnson doesn't know what the hell he's doing."

"Well, we have to fight the Communists some place," my father'd say. "If we don't stop 'em there, the next thing you know, they'll be attacking Pearl Harbor like the Japs did."

"Aw, come off it," my brother'd say. "Who are you afraid of? They're just fighting about their own country. It's a civil war."

"But if our president says we have to fight to defend these people, then we should fight."

"The president is a fool," my brother would say, and then my father would get really mad. "The whole government is corrupt. They've been lying about the war all along. They just want to kill off all us kids. That's why they're sending all the kids over there."

"And what would you do if they drafted you?" my father asked one day.

"I'd go to Canada," my brother said.

"You'd betray your country? You'd be a traitor?"

"The country is wrong. The war is immoral."

By that time, my father would just kind of shake his head. Then he'd start rubbing his forehead the way he usually did when he got upset. My father probably rubbed his forehead more times during that one week than he ever had in all his prior days.

One day they talked about a war protest demonstration my brother had gone to. "Yeah, I cut classes to go," my brother said.

"We're paying our hard-earned money to send you to college, and you spend your time cutting classes to protest our government," my father said, rubbing his forehead.

"The government is corrupt. They are hiding the truth," my brother said. "All they care about is making money."

It was bad. I started to feel bad for my father. My brother was criticizing everything he believed in. I sat at the table and listened, but I didn't know what to say. I always wanted to defend my brother, but I sure didn't want to go hurting my father's feelings any more than my brother was already doing. I really didn't know who was right, but I could sure as heck see that neither one wanted to give in.

Things were just bad all over.

My brother said he was working on a presidential campaign for a guy named Eugene McCarthy. He was an old guy with white hair who told jokes and stuff. My brother said Eugene McCarthy had made President Johnson drop out of the race. I told my brother I'd seen old LBJ on TV the night he said he was not going to seek a second term as president, but he didn't say it was because of Eugene McCarthy. The president looked real tired that night, and I kind of felt sorry for him. What with everybody yelling at him and criticizing him and all the protests and stuff, I could see why he wouldn't want to be president again. He said he wanted to devote the rest of his term to getting peace in Vietnam. He didn't mention ole Eugene McCarthy. I asked my brother if Eugene McCarthy was the one who'd gotten everybody in trouble for being Communists back in the 1950s and if he was the one who'd gotten Richard Nixon his start.

"What are you—a dummy or something?" my brother said. "It was *Joseph* McCarthy who did all the witch-hunting for Communists. What are they teaching you in school anyway? And old crazy Joe McCarthy got Bobby Kennedy his start, not Nixon."

I didn't say anything, but that surprised me and made me feel pretty darn lousy. I knew that Joe McCarthy was a totally despicable guy from learning about him in history class, but I sure hadn't known Bobby Kennedy was involved with him. I was really pissed off by what my brother had said, and I wanted to defend ole Bobby.

"Well, if I could vote, I'd be voting for Bobby Kennedy," I said, and I meant it.

"Bobby Kennedy? Ha!" my brother said, and my blood started to boil. "Why did he wait so long to decide to run? So he could let McCarthy take all the chances and knock LBJ out of the picture? Yeah, I used to like Bobby Kennedy but not anymore."

My blood slowly stopped boiling, but I was real hurt, and I felt lousy. I felt kind of the way my father did when he got into arguments with my brother. My brother just seemed to know everything. I really couldn't argue with him because he seemed to have all the facts, so what the heck could I say? But I still liked Bobby Kennedy, and nothing my brother could say would change that. I remembered how Bobby had talked to a crowd of angry people the night the Doc was shot and had tried to calm everybody. He'd tried to tell black people that white people were just as upset when Dr. King was killed. Bobby tried to smooth out the racial tensions. The other night, I'd seen him giving a speech, and he told some jokes too. They were a lot funnier than Eugene McCarthy's jokes, which nobody could understand anyway. I knew Jonathan liked Bobby too because he said black folks could always trust a Kennedy. I didn't say any of that to my brother.

Then my brother said, "Yeah, too bad Bobby isn't like his brother Jack. Jack was a good guy. We lost a lot when Jack was killed. Too bad Bobby can't be like his older brother."

That got me super pissed off, and I stomped out of the room. I thought, *Older brothers just stick together.* I decided right then that I was for Bobby all the way, no matter what anybody said.

My brother was leaving on Sunday afternoon, and I was still hoping maybe we could have some kind of a good time together, so on Friday night, I asked him if he'd like to go over to the stadium to see the Yanks.

"The Yanks, huh?" my brother said. "They gonna be any good this year? Or are they gonna stink up the league like last year?"

"Well, yeah, sure," I said. "They're gonna be good this year." Of course, I wasn't sure about that. I could see that we were headed for another argument.

"So who's gonna be good this year?" my brother asked.

"Ah, well, they say Pepitone's gonna have his best year ever."

"Pepitone?" My brother was not impressed. "He's a bum. Always was and always will be."

"Well, they've got Horace Clarke. He had a good year last year."

"Horace Clarke?" My brother started laughing. Then he shook his head in disgust and quietly said, "Horace Clarke." Then he spoke up a little louder, almost pleading. "It's never gonna be the same without Kubek and Richardson, Ellie and Yogi, Roger and the Moose. All the great guys are gone."

I perked up and said, "Well, they've still got the Mick."

"The Mick," my brother said quietly, almost somberly. "Yeah. The Mick." My brother shook his head and rubbed his chin. "The greatest player I ever saw, but what did he hit last year? Two forty-five?"

"Yeah. Well, he'll come back," I said. "His legs get lots of rest playing first base." I was pretty optimistic.

"Yeah, well, let me tell you something, T. J." My brother seemed sad and serious. "The Mick is washed."

"What?" I said. Of all the things my brother had said while home, including all the arguments with our parents and the stuff about Bobby Kennedy, nothing had made me feel worse than when he said those four words. I couldn't believe my brother could even think such a thing. Maybe our country was corrupt and all that, and maybe we should protest, grow our hair long, yell at our parents, listen to crazy music, and criticize people like Bobby Kennedy, but to say that the Mick was washed up was more than I could take. I was devastated.

"What are you—crazy?" I screamed. "He's got plenty of years ahead of him. He's still in great shape!"

"Hey, look, T. J., don't get all bent out of shape about your hero. Heck, he was my hero too. I loved the guy. But I'm just trying to tell you the truth. He's washed. It's over. He'll be lucky if he lasts the whole year before he retires. The guy was the greatest, but his legs are shot."

I became enraged. I wanted to belt my brother one. I knew I couldn't argue this one. All I could do was start cursing and screaming at him. I kicked over some furniture in our room and threw stuff. I did stuff I hadn't even done when I was a bratty little squirt.

I screamed, "You're wrong! What do you know? You creep!" Then I slammed the door, tore down the stairs, and ran outside. I got on my bike and just started riding. I rode and rode. I didn't get home until after dark. I didn't care when my parents said they'd been worried sick. I didn't talk to them, and I didn't talk to my brother. I didn't talk to my brother on Saturday, and I made sure I wasn't around when he left for college on Sunday.

CHAPTER 12

# Somebody Always Gets the Good Ones: Part 2

As the season went on, our team continued to play mediocre ball. We'd win a game and then lose a game. Then we'd win a game and lose two. By the middle of May, we were 6–9, and the coach wasn't too happy about it. We were not exactly a well-knit group either. Ever since the Doc's assassination, the riots in school, and the fights and stuff, we'd been divided between white kids and black kids. Our team was roughly half white and half black, and even before the racial problems, most of the white kids had stuck with the white kids, and the black kids had struck with the black kids, but at least on the field and in practice, we all used to get along all right. However, since all the trouble, there was hardly any team spirit or camaraderie. Jonathan still wasn't talking to me or to anybody who was white.

The whole season was a drag. Worse yet, I still had not done anything to distinguish myself at shortstop, and my mediocre play was one of the reasons we were such a mediocre team. Even though I was hitting under .250 right-handed, my confidence was at such a low level that I didn't want to buck my coach's wishes and try batting lefty. My fielding was still pretty sporadic, and sometimes I would make a really good play one inning and then totally botch one the next inning. To make matters worse, Darrell had just about recovered from his injuries.

We had a big game against Mayfield, and I knew I had better do something good, or else Darrell was sure to take over at shortstop. The game was on a Monday afternoon, so I decided to ride over to the baseball batting cages that Sunday to try to get in a little extra batting practice. The batting cages were out on the highway, and I had always wanted to go there, but it was a bit dangerous to get there on my bike. However, I figured the extra practice was necessary for me this time, so I took the chance and headed out there.

The cost was a quarter for nine pitches, and I wasn't exactly rolling in dough, but I did have a couple of bucks, so I changed them for eight quarters and set myself up in one of the batting cages. The stupid mechanical arm was extremely wild, and I got as many bad pitches as good pitches, but since I only got a limited number of pitches, I wanted to swing at everything. So I swung at everything. By my sixth quarter, I started to hit the ball better. I made a few adjustments in my stance and tried not to step in the bucket all the time. I was tempted to try batting lefty, and sure enough, I couldn't resist, so I got up lefty. I dragged a few bunts and slapped a few grounders to left field. *What a shame. If I could only get a few chances batting lefty, I could show the coach that I'm a pretty tough out.* I shook my head. I knew there was no way I was going to get up lefty in a game. I was just about to be replaced by Darrell anyway, and there was no way I wanted to antagonize the coach.

I was down to my last quarter, and I decided I'd try another machine. I hoped it would throw more good pitches. Sure enough, the new machine pitched nine beautiful strikes, and I got good swings and hit the ball hard just about every time. There was a net pretty far out there to stop the balls, and I even hit the net a few times. I was really feeling good about my hitting, but unfortunately, I had run out of money. However, just as I was putting away the bat, I heard a thud. I turned around and noticed that the machine was still pitching. Evidently, it was busted or something and didn't know how to turn off. Well, I didn't want to waste that opportunity, so I picked up the bat and got right back up there, swinging away and hitting the ball better than I had all season. After the nine pitches, the machine paused for a bit, and I was just about to put the bat away, but then it started pitching again—all strikes too. I took nine more good cuts and hit the ball really well. I even hit the net a few more times. I was starting to sweat, and after the nine extra pitches, I stepped aside to see if the machine would keep pitching. Sure enough, it started up again. I went right back up there, swinging away. What an opportunity it was—an endless amount of pitches with nobody waiting on deck like in practice, no coach yelling at me, and no complaints by the pitcher that he was getting tired. It was just pitch after pitch, strike after strike, and, the way I was swinging, base hit after base hit. I felt as if I had finally cured myself of my bad habit of stepping in the bucket, and furthermore, I was building up my confidence. Because I was right-handed and was stronger when batting righty, I found that when batting right-handed, I had more power, and I was actually hitting the ball pretty far. Then I started to notice that my left hand was hurting. I could see that I was developing blisters. I figured I should stop before the blisters got any worse, but I couldn't give up that great opportunity. It was like a baseball player's dream. I had never had so many pitches, and since there was probably nothing in the world I liked better than hitting a baseball, I just couldn't stop.

Finally, when my left hand was really starting to hurt and the blisters started to bleed, I called it quits. I remembered reading that Ted Williams used to take batting practice until his hands were bleeding, and I felt proud of myself. Best of all, I was more confident in my ability to hit than I had been all season.

The game was at Mayfield, so as usual when we had an away game, we got out of school early. That was one of the best advantages of being on the baseball teams. When we had an away game, they had to let us out early to catch the bus to the away school. I always felt totally cool getting up in the middle of the last-period class and giving my pass to the teacher, and out I went. *What status.* Well, I was psyched about the Mayfield game. I was raring to go. It was a pretty long ride to Mayfield, which was out in the sticks, so we didn't get to the field until a quarter to four. Since it was that late, we had no opportunity to take batting practice. Without batting practice, I didn't notice the problem until I was on deck for my first time at bat. As I took a few practice swings, I discovered that old Ted Williams mustn't have had important games on the days after he took batting practice until his hands bled, or maybe he was made of better stuff than I was, because my hands hurt so much from the blisters that when I gripped the bat, I could hardly swing. I got a sick feeling in my stomach that somehow I had blown it. What a jerk I was. There I was, brimming with confidence from my hours of batting practice, but I couldn't even hold a bat.

There was one out, and Gorski was on second with a double. I stepped to the plate and decided I was going to be tough just like Ted Williams. I swung at the first pitch, and my left hand hurt so much that I had to let go of the bat. The bat went sailing out toward shortstop. As I went out to get the bat, I heard somebody on the bench say, "Hey, look. The Wrecker's just as wild throwing a bat as he is a ball."

*Real funny.* I felt pretty darn embarrassed, but I was a heck of a lot more worried than embarrassed. This was probably my most important game ever, and I was not even able to swing a bat. I took the next two pitches, one for a ball and one for a strike. I swung at the next pitch and hit a weak grounder to the first baseman, and boy, did my hand hurt. The contact of ball to bat to blister made me see stars. I tried not to show the pain and headed over to a far corner of the bench. I didn't want to tell anybody, because it had been extremely stupid on my part to let myself get a hand full of blisters. I also didn't want to seem like a crybaby or an excuse maker, so I kept my mouth shut.

Big Billy came over to me and sarcastically said, "Nice hit, buddy. Maybe you'd better start aiming your bat at Darrell if you hope to keep your job."

"Thanks a lot, Billy," I said.

It was even tough out in the field. Every time I caught a ball, the blisters hurt like crazy. My next time up, I was afraid to swing because not only did it hurt to swing; it hurt twice as much when I made contact. I was lucky that the first two pitches were balls, and I hoped that maybe I could draw a walk. I took the next pitch, but it was a strike. The next one was a ball, so I had a 3–1 count. I was leading off the inning, so it was a good idea to try to get a walk, but I had no such luck. The next pitch was a strike, and so was the next. I looked at both and never took the bat off my shoulder. I walked slowly back to the bench and really heard it from the coach.

"Take the bat off your shoulder! You can't get a hit if you don't swing. Jeez! What—are you afraid you might hurt your hands or something?"

I wanted to say, "Yeah, Coach, you moron, that's exactly right."

Well, as the game went on, I felt pretty darn bad because it seemed as if everybody else was hitting the ball all over the place—on both sides. By the top of the fifth inning, when I came up for my third at bat, the score was 8–7. We were behind. Gorski was on third this time after a run-scoring triple. I really hoped the coach would call for the squeeze sign. With the way I was swinging, I hoped he would see that it would be best for me to bunt. Oh, how I wished I could have gotten up there lefty, dragged a nice little bunt down the first-base line, knocked in the tying run, and then beat out the play for a bunt single. But of course, there was no way I would ever buck the coach's order, especially in situation like that. How I wished I had never met up with the pitching machine that wouldn't stop. I took the first pitch, which was right down the middle for a strike. I could hear the coach yell, "Swing the darn bat!" I took feeble swings at the next two pitches and missed them both. I went over to the far corner of the bench and sat down. Even Big Billy wouldn't come over to say anything to me.

By the time the seventh inning rolled around, we were down 13–10. I was scheduled to bat third that inning. I went over to the first-aid kit, pulled out a can of Band-Aids, and put some on over the blisters. While I was doing that, I noticed Darrell had picked up a bat. My heart sank. The first two guys got on base, and I was due up. I had a bat in my patched-up hands, but the coach said, "Put the bat down, T. J. Darrell, get up there, and see if you can hit the ball."

I felt positively miserable, but I had to admit that deep down, I felt relieved. I knew I wasn't going to be able to hit the ball with my blistered hands, and I figured it was just as well to let Darrell get a chance. Sure enough, ole Darrell got up there and blasted a double into left-center field. Two runs scored. Darrell eventually came around to score, and we went ahead 15–13. The players went crazy. It was the first time in ages that there had been any spirit on the team. I had to admit I did feel kind of good for the team and for Darrell, but most of all, I felt relieved. We went on to win the game 15–14, and at least I didn't have to worry about being the goat. But that was Itsville for me.

I didn't start a game for the rest of the season.

Darrell did pretty well at shortstop, but really, over all he wasn't that great anyway. Darrell hit with really good power, and occasionally, he'd belt a long one, but he struck out a lot because he swung so hard. In the field, he definitely had a better arm than I did, and he threw overarm, which the coach loved, but he booted a lot more grounders than I ever did. And of course, Darrell was a hot dog and a loud mouth, and after a while, most of the kids on the team couldn't stand him, even the black kids.

I was disappointed at sitting on the bench, but at least I was relaxed. I didn't have to listen to the coach chew me out, and I didn't have to get nervous before games. I got to pinch-hit a few more times during the season after my blisters healed, and I got a few base hits. It was a lot easier to hit when I wasn't fighting for a job. I just got up there and swung away. I had made some improvements in my batting stance thanks to my time at the batting cages, so I felt good up at bat. Eventually, the coach started yelling at Darrell like he yelled at everybody. He kept getting on Darrell for swinging at bad pitches. Darrell was a free swinger up at the plate. That was his style. Sometimes he'd really blast the ball, and sometimes he'd miss it, sort of like the Mick or any power hitter. Well, the coach really would get on Darrell, and I could see that Darrell was starting to boil. Knowing Darrell, I figured he was set to explode, but when, none of us knew.

By the time June rolled around, things were sort of back to normal at school. The school had replaced the police officers with security guards. School was pretty darn boring, and with Jonathan still in mourning or whatever it was, things were boring in all my classes. Jonathan still wasn't talking to me or, as much as I could tell, anybody who was white. We had made plans way back in March to go to a twi-night doubleheader at the stadium, between the Yanks and the California Angels. We were pretty much stuck on doubleheaders because one game just wasn't enough, and we thought a twi-nighter would be neat, so as soon as the new 1968 Yankee schedule had come out, I'd sent away for four tickets. Boy, how things had changed.

Phil, Frankie, and Jonathan had agreed to go, and they had all paid their money way back when I'd sent for the tickets. Now Frankie was spending his Friday nights at Murray's stupid parties, Phil was spending all his time studying, and Jonathan wasn't even talking to me.

Well, it wasn't too much trouble to get Frankie's assurance that he would go once I reminded him that he'd paid for the ticket. Frankie wasn't one to throw away money, and he figured there would be plenty more parties at Murray's. Phil was easier to convince than I expected. In fact, he had never forgotten about the games and was looking forward to a chance to put down the books. Jonathan was another story. He still didn't want anything to do with me, so I figured there was no way he'd want to go.

The Tuesday before the Yankee twi-nighter, we had a game at home against Ridgeway. We lost 5–4. I didn't care that much. Darrell played a typical game for him. He hit two long doubles and struck out twice. The trouble was, the two times he struck out, he left men in scoring position. The coach wasn't too happy about that. I sat on the bench for the entire game. Jonathan sat on the bench too but down at the other end. After the game, I was one of the first to leave the locker room. There wasn't any need for me to take a stupid shower. Back home, I followed my same old routine: eat supper, do some homework, and then, at eight o'clock, put on the Yankees game. The Yanks looked totally pathetic losing to the Minnesota Twins, and the Mick was feeble—hitless in four at bats. *What a waste.* I hit the sack early, and I kind of wished I'd never gotten up that morning.

When I got up the next morning, as soon as I went downstairs, I could see that something was wrong. I heard the television, and my first thought was about the astronauts. My father always liked to turn on the TV in the morning when there was going to be a launch. I always thought they were pretty boring. Back when I was a little squirt in grammar school, when NASA would send up a rocket, the teachers would bring all the classes into the gym, and we would watch the takeoff on one of the two big TVs. However, the launch would always be delayed, and we'd get bored while sitting around waiting. When the rocket took off, we could hardly see anything more than a speck on the screen, but we could always hear old Walter Cronkite going on and on about how great the takeoff was and everything. It seemed like a waste to watch it, and I thought the teachers had us watch it so they could get out of teaching for a few hours.

It didn't take long for me to realize that what was on the TV wasn't a dopey space launch, and how I wished it was.

My father was sitting on the couch in his work clothes, rubbing his forehead like he did when he was upset. On the TV, some guy was giving a news report outside a hospital, talking about somebody who had been shot. My father shook his head and said, "They got another one. Somebody always gets the good ones."

Then the newsman started talking about Bobby Kennedy, and I felt a chill go down my spine. I heard the newsman say, "Senator Robert Kennedy lies gravely wounded, shot in the head by an unnamed gunman."

I said, "Oh no!" or something lame like that. Then my father started going on about how they always got the good ones, and he let out a long sigh, all while he kept rubbing his forehead.

My mother came in, holding back tears. "Don't say that. He'll be all right. We just have to pray." Then she said, "T. J., go eat your breakfast," but I wasn't really listening.

I could feel my stupid face quivering, and all of a sudden, I had to tear upstairs to my room. I felt like a jerk, but I started crying and couldn't stop. I cried like

I was some dim-witted little squirt. I just couldn't stand the thought of Bobby Kennedy being shot—just like his brother. I tried to imagine what it would be like to be shot. People were always getting shot up on stupid TV shows, but they never showed much blood or anything, except maybe in the movies. In *Bonnie and Clyde*, there was blood all over when they got shot. But this was a real live person, a person lots of people really cared about—a guy who wanted to be president and help people out. He wanted to help fix things between blacks and whites and stop all the violence and rioting, and now he'd been shot. He wanted to stop the stupid war in Vietnam so young soldiers would stop getting killed, and people wouldn't have to spend so much time arguing about it. Bobby was a good guy. He was good looking and even had his hair kind of long like my brother's. But now Bobby had been shot in the head and gravely wounded. It didn't make any sense.

I turned on the radio by my bed and switched to a station with the news. The reporter said Bobby was in stable but critical condition, and the doctors didn't know if he could pull through. He said that people all over the country were praying for the senator, so I said a quick prayer, and I figured maybe there was still hope after all. I eventually got up. I had a glass of juice to please my mother and went to school.

Things seemed a little quieter than normal, and some of the kids were whispering about the shooting. Our history teacher canceled his regular lesson and devoted the entire class to a discussion about violence in America.

It was a really good discussion because our town had already had its share of violence. I didn't say much because I was still pretty darn upset, but the discussion was good. We talked about how there were loads of guns in our country, and despite the fact that JFK and the Doc had been gunned down, there were still no gun-control laws. The class thought that was pretty lame. Our teacher, Mr. Fisher, said even after this assassination attempt, there still probably wouldn't be any meaningful gun-control laws. We all thought Mr. Fisher was being kind of cynical, and then I had to open my big mouth by saying that when Bobby Kennedy got better, he'd make sure some laws were passed.

Mr. Fisher wasn't so sure. "Ah, the idealism of youth," he said. "And maybe you're right. But have you ever heard of the National Rifle Association?" He went on about that group of people, who thought everybody should be able to have a gun. Then Mr. Fisher said something that really made me feel sick.

"But you know, T. J.," he said, "the ironic part of it all—and the most tragic aspect of the youthful idealism you expressed—is that the only leader with enough of that youthful idealism, energy, and dedication to do something about it is lying flat on his back in a hospital in Los Angeles with a gunshot wound in his head. And frankly, T. J., even if Bobby Kennedy survives, he'll never be the same person. The brain damage he suffered has been so extensive that even if he lives, it will probably be as nothing more than a vegetable."

I felt I was about to start crying again, but I also felt nauseated. Fortunately, the class ended, and I made an emergency trip to the bathroom. I couldn't get the thought out of my mind. *Bobby Kennedy—a vegetable.* I really felt sick. Somehow, I made it through the day okay, but I cut baseball practice. It was the first time I had missed practice all year, but I didn't feel up to running around and playing baseball. I went home and listened to the radio in the backyard because it was too hot up in my room. Around suppertime, there was a report that Bobby was in critical condition, but his heart was still pumping. Bobby had undergone a three-hour operation, and the bullets had been removed. There would be no more reports until the morning, so I turned off the radio.

My parents were both kind of subdued, so they didn't bother me much with idle chitchat, which was just as well. I watched a little of the news reported by good old Walter Cronkite, who looked solemn and seemed positively depressed as he talked about the shooting. Walter looked a whole lot better when he announced those space launches. It was all too depressing, so I went upstairs, where I watched the Yanks on TV and then went to bed. I said as many dopey prayers for Bobby as I could think of.

When I woke up the next morning, I turned on my radio. I was anxious to hear the latest news, but then I thought, *What if it's bad?* It was bad. Early that morning, Bobby Kennedy had died.

I was too sad to even cry about it. I didn't feel like going to school, but I went anyway. I didn't say anything to anybody. I felt real sad but didn't feel like crying any more, or maybe I just couldn't anymore. When I got to biology class, Jonathan came up to me, looking serious, and said, "I heard on the news this morning that they're going to bring Bobby Kennedy's body to St. Patrick's Cathedral in New York City on Friday to lie in state. I think we should stop by there and pay our respects before we go to the twi-nighter." I didn't know what to say. I was surprised Jonathan was talking to me, but I couldn't understand what he was talking about. I had never heard of St. Patrick's Cathedral, and Jonathan mentioned it as if he went there all the time. I wasn't sure what he meant by "lying in state," but I figured that was what they did when a famous American died. I guessed it was part of the grieving process.

"I wish I had gone to the Doc's funeral," Jonathan said, "but it was way too far away. I wish I could have paid my respects to the Doc. But I guess that's how it goes."

I didn't want to make a big deal out of Jonathan talking to me, and I was caught so off guard that all I could say was "Yeah, okay, Jonathan." I stared at him for a long time. He didn't smile. He wasn't scowling either. He just had a dead-serious expression.

Jonathan didn't talk to me for the rest of the day. I didn't really have anything to say to anybody, but as the day wore on, I began to feel a little better. I thought maybe it would be neat to pay my respects to Bobby Kennedy. I figured that was what you did when somebody you cared about died. Just thinking about doing it kind of made me feel better. Of course it was something Jonathan would think of. Did that mean we were friends again now that we were even?

I got ahold of Phil, and he said it would be all right with him if we stopped off to pay our respects. I told Frankie, but Frankie wasn't too keen on the idea. He said he'd always liked Bobby Kennedy because he had long hair and liked to climb mountains and stuff, and Bobby wasn't an old stuffed shirt like LBJ or Richard Nixon. But then I told Frankie that if we went to the cathedral, we'd have to leave at about noon and cut our afternoon classes. Frankie's eyes lit up, and he said, "Now you're talking. Yeah. Come to think of it, I always do feel it's a good idea to pay your respects to the dead—especially when you do it on school time."

Friday was a nice day—bright, sunny, and warm. I felt a lot better about things. It seemed as if we were headed on another of Jonathan's adventures. We'd be heading into New York, and I had no idea where the heck we'd be. Jonathan would be leading the way—just like old times. I told my parents we'd be going to St. Patrick's Cathedral to pay our respects to Bobby Kennedy before the Yankees games, and my mother didn't seem to care. As a matter of fact, it seemed she thought it was a good idea. Of course, I acted as if I knew right where St. Patrick's Cathedral was, as if I went there every week or so to catch a quick novena. My mother said, "Say a little prayer for me." I didn't think she really cared that much about Bobby, but I thought that if she had had the chance, she would have gone down to Washington to pay her respects to JFK during his funeral. My mother didn't care much about politics, and whatever she had cared about had faded away when JFK died.

We took the New York bus from downtown and made it to the Port Authority in a little less than an hour. When we got off the bus, Jonathan, of course, took the lead, as he always did, and this time, none of us had any idea where the heck he was going, so we made sure we stayed right behind him. It wasn't that hard this time because Jonathan wasn't going at his usual breakneck speed—I guessed because we really didn't have any deadline, since it was only about one fifteen, and we had until five before game time. I also thought Jonathan was holding back because of the somberness of the occasion. We all were a bit excited about cutting school and being in the big city, but Jonathan remained somber, and he kind of set the tone for our day. As we went down grimy Forty-Second Street, Jonathan made no attempt to check out any peep shows, even though Frankie tried to get us to stop.

"Hey, we've got all afternoon," Frankie said. Jonathan stopped and gave Frankie one of his best scowls. "All right, all right," Frankie said. "I know it's not appropriate for this somber occasion."

We headed on up through the city. When we got to Times Square, we made a left and headed up Seventh Avenue. It was hot, so of course, Frankie wanted to stop for an Italian ice.

"It's okay on such a somber occasion, isn't it?" Frankie asked Jonathan sarcastically. Jonathan gave another scowl. Phil bought one too, but I stuck to Jonathan's code of abstention.

We passed a go-go bar that advertised "Hottest Lunchtime Dancers." Frankie stopped and said, "Hey, I'm getting real hungry." Then he tried to look through the partially open door. Jonathan didn't even turn around to scowl but seemed to speed up his pace. I stopped and went back to get Frankie.

"Come on, you maniac," I said. "Jonathan's the only one who knows where the heck we're going."

"Yeah? Well, I think *he's* the maniac," Frankie said.

"Come on," I said as we turned to head up Seventh Avenue. We saw no sign of Jonathan or Phil. The street was crowded with people, and I dodged around, looking for Jonathan.

"Hey, T. J., buddy," Frankie said, "don't go panicking. I know my way around the city like the back of my hand."

"Sure, Frankie," I said. "Like the time you almost got lost forever in the subways until Jonathan rescued you."

"Hey, that was below ground. I'm an above-ground person. I ain't no mole, you know, and besides, I wasn't really lost down there, just a little confused. You know, there's no stars or heavenly bodies down there to guide you. Speaking of heavenly bodies!" Frankie stopped to check out some girl in a miniskirt.

"Cool it, Frankie," I said. "Let's go."

We got to Fiftieth Street and still saw no sign of Jonathan, but I heard Phil yell, "Hey, come on!" He was waving for us. We ran to catch up with Phil.

"Where's Jonathan?" I said.

"He's up ahead." Phil pointed. "See him over there? I don't know what got into him, but he's really moving, and he won't stop for nothing."

"Well, let's go," I said, and the three of us took off after Jonathan.

When we crossed the street, we lost sight of Jonathan. I was ready to panic, but Phil seemed to have things under control.

"I think he went thata way," Phil said, and he pointed up Fiftieth Street. We headed up the block.

When we got to the corner, Frankie yelled, "Holy smokes! Look at that!"

There it was: St. Patrick's Cathedral, the biggest darn church I had ever seen in my life. I was no expert on churches, but it was one heck of an impressive sight.

"Hey, I wouldn't even mind going to church if our church looked like that," Frankie said.

"You Catholics sure do get carried away with your religion." Phil had to put in his two cents.

We crossed the street, and there was Jonathan. "Well, you boys finally made it," he said. "And I see Frankie didn't get lost."

"Don't get smart, Jonathan," Frankie said. "So what was the big rush for?"

"Look." Jonathan pointed to the front steps of the cathedral. A trail of people went up the stairs and through the immense doors.

"So big deal. There's a little line," Frankie said. "Let's go hop in line."

"Be my guest," Jonathan said, and he let Frankie lead the way. As we made our way to the front of the cathedral, we saw that the line trailed out and up toward Fifty-First Street and turned the corner. We turned the corner, and there was the line. Frankie swung out toward the street to see if he could find the end of the line, but it was nowhere in sight.

"Holy macaroni!" Frankie said. We followed the line down that street and up the next street and up and down several streets until we finally got to the end.

"This is absolutely amazing," Phil said in the understatement of the year.

"I can't believe how long this line is," I said.

"Holy macaroni," Frankie said.

It was the longest line I had ever seen. It reminded me of some of the lines at the World's Fair, but even they were not nearly as long as this one was, and at least at the end of those lines, you got to go on some neat rides. Here, we were just going to church.

Despite all our amazement, Jonathan remained silent. When he finally did say something, he said, "The line for the Doc down in Atlanta was just about as long." I didn't know how the heck Jonathan could know how long the line was for the Doc, but I guessed Jonathan had his own way to calculate.

As we took our place at the end of the line, Frankie went out to the curb and looked up ahead. "Holy macaroni with marinara sauce," Frankie said. The line was moving slowly but decently. I had no idea where we were headed or how the heck we would get to our destination. I guessed only Jonathan had any idea about that. It was about two o'clock, and we tried to estimate how long the line would take. We had another destination, and I, for one, sure as heck didn't want to miss a chance to see the Mick in a twi-nighter. Of course, I was fully prepared to miss a few innings if I had to in order to pay my respects.

Most of the people in the line were solemn, but after a while, we noticed some people yakking away. We even heard a few chuckles here and there as people accepted the fact that they were in for quite a wait. Of course, Frankie didn't know what it meant to be solemn, so it didn't take him long to start getting into a conversation with Phil about sports. Soon enough, Frankie found something to argue with Phil about, and as usual, Frankie didn't know what the heck he was talking about. He was trying to convince Phil that Joe Pepitone could hit the great Dodger pitcher Sandy Koufax with his eyes closed and that Sandy Koufax was a bum for retiring so young. It didn't take long before Phil got tired of Frankie's cockeyed logic, so he just ignored Frankie. However, some guy just up ahead who'd overheard the conversation evidently took offense to Frankie mean-mouthing ole Sandy Koufax. The guy said he was from Brooklyn and remembered the day Sandy Koufax had broken into the majors. I could see that Frankie had met his match, but would Frankie back down? Of course not. He went on and on, getting more ridiculous about how overrated Sandy Koufax was. Then Frankie really stuck his foot in his mouth when he said that Sandy Koufax was a chump for not pitching a World Series game on a Jewish holiday. Well, the guy from Brooklyn happened to be Jewish too, and I thought he was just about ready to strangle Frankie, but he backed off when Phil and I stepped in between them.

"Hey, look. Don't worry about this guy," I said to the Jewish Dodgers fan from Brooklyn. "Ah, he really doesn't know what he's talking about." That, of course, was true.

Then Jonathan chimed in, using his best blacknosing voice. "Yes, sir. The young boy, unfortunately, has a mental disability."

Frankie got pretty pissed off at that, but Phil put his hand over Frankie's mouth, and we dragged him back behind Jonathan.

"Yeah, sir. He has a mental disability, sir," I said. It kind of felt nice to tell somebody that Frankie was crazy, since he was always getting in trouble and acting as if he were crazy.

"Vell, ya shunta bring him out if he's dat vay," the Brooklyn guy said. "Sheesh. Talking about da great Koufax like dat!"

Come to think of it, maybe the Brooklyn guy wasn't all there either.

Once we had Frankie under control and things had calmed down, the wait started to get a little boring. It was two thirty, and St. Patrick's Cathedral was nowhere in sight—and it was a pretty darn big place to lose sight of. Frankie and Phil were getting restless, so they started to set deadlines. They agreed that three thirty was the latest they'd wait because they wanted to get to the stadium in time to see a little batting practice. I wasn't going to commit myself to a deadline, and Jonathan remained stoic and somber and did not even participate in the discussion.

It was getting hot. On some streets, we'd be in the shade of a skyscraper or something, but then we'd turn a corner and would be in the sun for what seemed like hours. Fortunately, there were places where some people gave out water. We called them water stations, and it sure was good to have something to drink. Of course, Frankie wasn't satisfied with just water. He wanted a soda. He and Phil got out of line, went over to a pushcart vendor, and bought four sodas. They gave one each to me and Jonathan, but Jonathan wouldn't take his.

"Water's fine for me," Jonathan said. "Thank you anyway." None of us could believe Jonathan would turn down a soda. He was a soda freak.

"What are you—loco, Senor?" Frankie said to Jonathan, using a silly Spanish accent.

We all slurped down our sodas, and Phil tried to give the extra soda away to a lady up ahead of us, but she declined. "What the heck—is this a funeral or something?" Frankie blurted out, and we all gave him looks of disgust. "Yeah, yeah, I know," Frankie said, and he took off one of his sneakers and put it in his mouth. "I might as well just keep this here," he mumbled.

I kind of felt guilty about drinking my soda, and the whole incident brought me back to reality. We weren't there to have fun or screw around; we were there because Bobby Kennedy was dead. In a way, it was actually nice that Frankie tried to liven things up a little, but I could see that this was different from a bunch of kids waiting in line to get tickets for a rock concert or a ball game. We were there to pay our respects to somebody a lot of people really cared about. It was a little scary when I thought about it. Just two months ago, a whole lot of people had been doing the same thing down in Atlanta, Georgia, and it hadn't been too many years since they were lining up in Washington, DC. I also thought about all the guys getting killed over in Vietnam. People were lining up to pay their respects all over the place.

At three thirty, we were still in line, and the cathedral was nowhere to be seen. Frankie and Phil started to hem and haw about leaving and heading to the stadium.

"Well, look, fellows," Frankie said, "all due respect to ole Bobby. He was really a great guy. But I got this here ticket in my wallet that cost three dollars and fifty cents, and I sure as heck don't want to let it go to waste."

"Yeah. Well, Frankie," Phil said, "we still have plenty of time. Let's give the line a little longer."

"But we'll miss all of batting practice," Frankie said.

"Look, Frankie," I said, "it's a twi-nighter. How much baseball do you want?"

"My money's worth."

"You're getting two for the price of one anyway," Phil said.

"I can't help it if the price of one game is overpriced," Frankie said.

"Well, I'm staying another half hour," Phil said. "What about you, T. J.?"

"At least a half hour."

"And you, Jonathan? You haven't had much to say."

"As long as it takes," Jonathan said seriously. We all got quiet and continued our slow journey.

The sun was blazing, and the people in line remained pretty quiet. There were crowd-control barriers and lots of police around, and the line stretched from block to block and street to street. Every once in a while, we'd see a portion of the line across the street, and we couldn't figure out how the heck it was connected to our part of the line. We couldn't tell whether that part was ahead of us or behind us. When four thirty rolled around, Frankie just about had had it.

"Okay, look. That's Itsville for me. I'm on my way. You guys can stay here all night if ya like. Take the A train to the D train. Right, Jonathan?"

"Not exactly," Jonathan said. "You take the A train to the D train from the Port Authority. Not from here."

"Oh yeah. Yeah," Frankie said. "I knew that."

"Sure, Frankie," I said with a smirk.

"Well, come on. You guys made a deal. You said a half hour more, T. J., more than an hour ago."

I didn't know what to say. I was torn.

"Yeah, you're right, Frankie," Phil said. "This wait may go on forever. I think we all did our part. Waiting in line for three hours should be enough respect paying. Let's get going. What do you say, T. J.? Jonathan?"

I didn't know what the heck to say, and I was kind of waiting for Jonathan to say something, but he was as stoic and somber as ever.

"Well, what'll it be, fellers?" Phil asked.

I kept waiting for Jonathan to lead the way. Then I said, "I'm staying."

"Staying?" Frankie said. "Come on, T. J., ole boy. You don't want to miss your boy, the Mick. You know, this could be his last year."

"Don't say that!" I snapped. Frankie knew how to get at me. "I'm staying. I have to stay. This is more important."

I wasn't sure why it was more important to stay in line for hours just to go by somebody's coffin, but somehow, deep in my heart, I knew it was. It was more important than some stupid baseball game. Bobby Kennedy had stood for a lot of things. He'd been trying to make the world better. The people in line—I guessed there were thousands—all felt the same way. I could watch the Mick anytime on television, but this was the end for Bobby. Tomorrow he'd be laid to rest next to his brother. No, I couldn't go to the game. I had to stay, and I knew Jonathan would too.

"I'm staying," I said again to Frankie and Phil.

"Well, I guess you're staying too," Phil said to Jonathan.

"Yep," Jonathan said.

"Well, could you at least give us a tip on how to get up to the stadium from here?" Phil said.

Jonathan went into a long, detailed explanation of how and where to catch the subway and what trains to take. It was the most he had talked all day.

"And, Phil," Jonathan said, nodding to Frankie, "please keep an eye on that one. The one with the mental disability."

"Hey, knock it off, Jonathan," Frankie said.

"I won't be around to rescue him," Jonathan added.

"Yeah, Phil. Keep an eye on him." I had to add my two cents.

"Yeah. Thanks, T.J.," Frankie said sarcastically. "Come on, Phil; it's getting later. Oh, and, you guys, enjoy the party."

They started away, but Frankie turned back, came over, and whispered to me, "Would you say a quick Hail Mary for me or something when you get there?"

"Yeah. Sure, Frankie," I said, and they left.

CHAPTER 13

# Maggie

It was past five o'clock when we crossed the street at Fifty-Fifth Street. A girl up in front of us asked me what time it was.

"Five fifteen," I said.

"Isn't it wonderful?" she said.

"Ah, what?" I asked.

"All these people," she said. "I mean, I know it's sad. Real, real sad. But isn't it wonderful that so many people really care? I mean, don't you sometimes think that nobody anywhere really cares about anything? Except normal everyday stuff—like what to wear to parties or a dance. But look at all these people. They really do care. Don't they?"

She finally stopped, and I guessed I was supposed to say something, but I wasn't sure what, so I just said, "Yeah. You're right."

"Wow. It's a beautiful sight," she said. "How long have you been here?"

"Since about one thirty," I answered.

"Yeah? That's just about the time my friend Diane and I got in line." The girl became enthusiastic.

I hadn't noticed her before, but I'd been too concerned with Frankie and deciding whether or not to stay. Sometimes it seemed that when we crossed the street or something, people got moved around a little in the line. It wasn't a tight single-file line or anything; it was the whole width of the sidewalk. But anyway, I had never noticed this girl or her friend.

"Um, this is my friend Diane. I'm Maggie," the girl said.

"Oh, hi," I said. "Um, I'm T. J., and this is my friend Jonathan."

Jonathan said hello. He asked the girls where they were from, and they said Bloomington. Then Jonathan started talking with Diane, and Maggie started talking to me.

"Are you in high school?" Maggie asked. "You probably are. What grade?"

"Tenth," I said.

"Tenth. Wow. Same with me. What did you think of Bobby Kennedy?" She didn't let me even try to answer before she went on. "I think he was a great man. Probably the best man this country has ever known. I know he would have changed the world. He could have, you know. He was going to stop this terrible war. My cousin was killed over there in Vietnam. He was just twenty-one years old. Nobody in our family will even talk about the way he died. But I know he got blown to bits. Nobody likes to think about it, and that's why nobody talks about it. But that's what happened to my cousin, his sister, says. She says her brother was blown to bits. She says nobody was allowed to look at the body or anything. And she says it's because there wasn't even any body left to put into the coffin. It was horrible. The whole war is horrible. And they don't even know why they are fighting. LBJ is a big dummy. You heard what they're singing about him: 'LBJ, how many kids have you killed today?' Well, I don't think even LBJ knows for sure. But Bobby would have put an end to it. So do you think there was a conspiracy?" Again, Maggie didn't wait for an answer before she went on. "I think so. I mean, just like when President Kennedy was killed. Now, you know that was a conspiracy. Well, I don't know who they were, but since nobody caught them, maybe they went and did another one. And they probably were the ones who killed Martin Luther King Jr."

"Yeah? Well, who was it?" I finally blurted out.

"Oh, I don't know," Maggie said quietly, and she didn't say anything for a few minutes. I tried to think of something to say to keep the conversation going, but then she asked, "Do you like the Beatles?"

"Um, I guess I do," I said.

"Yeah? Well, I do too. I like George. He's the cutest. But Paul's a lefty. I'm a lefty. Are you?"

"No. Righty all the way."

"Hmm," she said thoughtfully. "How about Diana Ross. Don't you think she's beautiful? And she has such a wonderful voice."

I didn't get a chance to answer before she had another question.

"You don't watch *The Mod Squad*, do you?"

"Ah, no."

"Good. I can't stand people who watch *The Mod Squad*, you know? I've got this one friend who thinks she's mod. I mean, she wears these miniskirts and goes out with this varsity football player. He's got a car—a Mustang. Do you think Mustangs are mod? I guess they're supposed to be. She and her varsity football player friend go to drive-ins and then hang out at Joe's Diner. I guess you don't know about Joe's Diner, but it's a real dive. But they don't kick the kids out, so a lot of kids hang out there. I guess it must be mod to hang out at Joe's Diner. And she puts so much ketchup on her hamburgers. So the ketchup always leaks out of the hamburger and drips on the plate in big globs. Is it mod to eat hamburgers with drippy ketchup?"

I got the feeling she really didn't expect me to answer all these questions. She seemed like one of those girls who, if you put an ear within five feet, would talk forever. But she seemed sincere. She had long light brown hair, soft brown eyes, and a sprinkle of freckles on her nose. When she looked at me, she seemed down to earth. She was really kind of nice.

"You say your name is T. J.? What's it stand for? Or am I prying? Don't you just love that phrase? 'Am I prying?' They always say that in the movies and on television: 'Am I prying?'" Every time she said, "Am I prying?" she kind of tilted her head back, like a movie star or something. "Well, T. J., let me give you a less personal question. Where do you live?" She said this with a movie star voice and then laughed.

"Rosedale."

"Oh yeah. Is that over by Newark anywhere?"

"Sort of," I said.

"Boy, did you see what went on in Newark last year? We always love shopping in Newark, but we were afraid there would disturbances all over again when Martin Luther King Jr. was assassinated. You know, my town is right next door, and we were all worried that the riots would spread on over to our town."

"We had a riot in our town," I said. I almost felt as if I were bragging or something. Then I told her about all the troubles we'd had at school and in town.

"That's horrible," Maggie said.

She seemed interested, and this time, I started talking her ear off, but she seemed to listen carefully. I even told her about Jonathan and how he wouldn't speak to me for two months. Jonathan was a bit up ahead of us, yakking away with Diane, so he couldn't overhear what I was saying. Maggie listened to everything. I even felt like telling her about our baseball team, but when I mentioned baseball, she said, "Baseball? Ooh. How boring. I like skiing. Jean-Claude Killy. Now, he's my man."

Well, you could count me out of any discussion of skiing because I knew nothing about it. I let her go on about her Jean-Claude Killy for a while and then about the Winter Olympics, which I personally thought was one of the most boring sporting events I had ever watched. Finally, when she was done, we both kind of took a breather and continued quietly with our journey. I had a new friend who, even though she liked something as boring as skiing, really cared about things, including ole Bobby Kennedy, and it warmed my heart. Seriously.

We crossed another street, but St. Patrick's Cathedral was still nowhere around. The sun had dipped down behind some skyscrapers, and we were now in the shade. Jonathan came over to me, and Diane came over to talk with Maggie.

"How'd it go over there?" Jonathan asked, and for the first time all afternoon, he seemed enthusiastic.

"Um, well, okay, I guess," I said.

"Well, I hope you appreciate my clearing out the side for you."

"Huh?" I said.

"Clearing out the side so you and Maggie could get to know each other. I think you're a perfect match."

"What? Come on."

"Clearing out the side" was another one of Jonathan's expressions. It came from basketball, when all the players on your team moved out of the way so you could go one on one with a player on the opposition.

"Well, it looked like you were doing pretty well over there," Jonathan said. "I think she likes you."

"Oh, come on, Jonathan." I felt embarrassed.

"And I bet you like her too," Jonathan said, and he gave me an elbow in the ribs.

"Oh, come on," I said, but as usual, Jonathan was right. Of course I liked Maggie. I didn't know too much about her, but she seemed to have an awful lot on the ball, even if she didn't like baseball.

"Yeah, well, T. J., buddy boy, make darn sure you get her address and phone number. Remember—name, address, and phone number." Then he went over to Diane. "Hey, Diane, did I tell you about the time I met Jimi Hendrix?" Jonathan then quickly turned around and mouthed, "Clearing out the side," and he made a motion as if he were throwing a basketball to me. Sure enough, Maggie wandered back over to me and started talking away.

"My parents don't know I'm here," she said. "Diane and I cut school to come over here. I think my mother wouldn't ever approve of us going into New York City alone, but I know she cared about Bobby, and I'm sure she'll understand when I get home."

I told Maggie about how my mother kind of had given me approval, and then I told her about all the times Jonathan, our friends, and I had come to New York, but I left out the peep show stories. She laughed when I told her about how dumb ole Frankie had gotten lost on the subways, and we both speculated about whether Frankie and Phil ever got to the stadium on their own.

"I wish I could come here more often," Maggie said.

"Hey, you want to come to see a ball game sometime?" I blurted out without really thinking. Then, all of a sudden, I got a sick feeling when I remembered that she'd told me she thought baseball was boring.

But she didn't hesitate. "Oh, wow. Yeah, sure. I'd love to."

There was a little bit of a silence. I felt a little embarrassed again.

Just then, we turned a corner, and there it was: St. Patrick's Cathedral. It wasn't the sort of thing I would have expected to sneak up on me, but sure enough, that was exactly what it did.

"My God. Look at that," Maggie said. A shaft of sunlight was shining on the steeple, and the rest of the church was in the late-afternoon shadows. The line headed up the steps and into the church. There were some police around the front of the cathedral, along with a lot more police barricades. I saw three or four TV cameras, with reporters and wires and microphones; a Channel 7 truck; a Channel 2 truck; a radio truck; and all kinds of people just standing around watching the line as it slowly made its way up the steps and into the cathedral. Despite all the people milling around all over, it was amazingly quiet and positively eerie. Even Jonathan, who had totally changed from his somber mood, stopped telling Diane all his stories and once again became silent.

Just then, Maggie got real close to me and whispered, "Isn't it beautiful? Isn't it just the most beautiful cathedral in the world? But isn't it sad? I mean, but isn't it *so* sad? Isn't it the saddest thing you ever saw in your whole life?" She started sobbing. Then she put her head on my shoulder for what seemed like forever but must have been only a few seconds. Then Maggie broke away from me and straightened up. "Hmm," she said. "I'd better get ahold of myself."

"It's okay," I said. It was just about seven o'clock, and I figured the whole first game was probably just about over. I wondered if maybe the Mick had hit one out. I thought maybe we'd be through in time to see the second game, but then I thought there was no way I'd even want to see the second game. I was too sad to be thinking about a stupid baseball game. I was just too darn sad.

By the time we got to the steps, it was eight o'clock, and the entire cathedral was in shadows. The line had squeezed into just two rows and was moving slowly. Jonathan called it a classic bottleneck. We took each step one at a time. The line had grown real quiet. When we finally entered the cathedral, I couldn't help but gasp at how immense the place was. Jonathan had arranged it so that he walked next to Diane, and I walked next to Maggie. I wasn't sure who he was clearing the side out for, me or himself, but when we stepped inside, Maggie grabbed ahold of my arm. She looked around in amazement too. I didn't think there were any churches as big as St. Patrick's in New Jersey. As we walked up the aisle, nobody said anything. Even Maggie didn't breathe a word, and Jonathan was back to his somberness. I could hear only the slow shuffling of hundreds of feet and an occasional cough that would echo throughout the whole place.

It seemed like the longest aisle in the world. I thought that people who got married in that church probably let the bride use a golf cart. I checked out all the religious stuff. It was all pretty much the standard equipment for any Catholic church, except this place had more of everything. Churches always felt somber and lonely to me, and it seemed this one magnified everything. It was just so big; it made me feel small and insignificant. I didn't think I'd ever want to go there alone—that would be downright spooky.

As we walked up the aisle, there was no sign of the casket, but we knew we had to be getting close. I was glad Jonathan was ahead of me because I had no idea what the heck I was supposed to do when I got to it. I could hear some people quietly sobbing, but nobody was going around screaming his or her head off. Jonathan once told me that at the funerals he went to, the women were expected to be screaming, yelling, and bawling away, and the most impressive thing the women could do was faint. He said one of his aunts held the record in his family for the most consecutive times fainting at a funeral: nine. He thought she was fully capable of double digits. His father had suggested she rent herself out for funerals. If some old geezer nobody cared about died, the family could hire Jonathan's aunt to faint at the funeral. It reflected badly on a family if somebody in the family was so disliked that nobody fainted at the funeral. Jonathan's aunt could have provided quite a service. She probably could have charged twenty-five dollars per faint and maybe offered a deluxe package that included some serious bawling for an additional ten dollars. Anyway, I didn't see anybody fainting or wailing. Everybody tried to keep his or her composure, but there sure as heck wasn't anybody smiling.

I could tell we were getting close to the casket because we were nearing the front of the church. I could see some people genuflecting. That was always a requirement when you reached the front of a church. Then I saw it: just off to the right was the casket. It seemed huge. Bobby wasn't such a big guy, so I was sure he had plenty of room in there. People would go up to the casket and touch it, and that was all. Some people made the sign of the cross. A few people had their rosary beads out, and I could see their lips moving. They were probably on their four millionth Hail Mary or something. Jonathan went first. He touched the coffin, and that was it. Diane touched the coffin and made the sign of the cross. Then they headed out to the right. One couldn't stay at the coffin for more than a few seconds. I mean, we knew there were thousands of people behind us, and we sure didn't want to slow up the works any more.

Maggie had hold of my arm as we got to the casket, and she wouldn't let go, so we went up to the coffin and touched it together. She let go of my arm for just a second as she made the sign of the cross, and then she grabbed back on. Her eyes were full of tears. Seeing her eyes filled with tears gave me a bad pang of sorrow. I wasn't really even thinking of Bobby anymore. He wasn't there. In front of this oversized, cold, sad-looking coffin in this oversized, sad ole church, I was thinking about Maggie. That this beautiful girl could be moved to tears really affected me. I tried my darnedest not to start sobbing myself. We walked over to the side of the church where the side exit was. Jonathan came up to me and grabbed my arm. He wasn't looking at me, so I didn't know whether he could see that I was on the verge of crying. He whispered in my ear, "I heard the Yanks won the first game."

"Yeah?" I said. "When did you hear that?"

Jonathan had gotten my mind off everything. "Just before we got into the church. Some guy told me. He had a transistor radio."

As Jonathan and I were whispering, Maggie and Diane went over to light a candle. I had never seen so many candles before in my life. The church must have hauled out an extra truckload to handle the heavy demand. Maybe some altar boy went around discreetly putting out some of the candles so there would always be a supply of unlit candles people could light. Of course, when you lit a candle, you were required to make a contribution in the coin box. The church must have made a mint from ole Bobby.

We left the church through the side exit. There were lots of bright lights from TV cameras, and we wondered if we were on television. It was about eight thirty, and Jonathan and I knew there was no way we would be going to the stadium for the second game. I was happy we had finished paying our respects, but I felt emotionally drained by the whole thing, and I didn't know what to do next. Maggie was still kind of somber, and I wished there was something I could do to perk her up. Then there was the matter of how to get back to the bus terminal—I had no idea where the heck we were. However, as usual, good old Jonathan had matters well in hand. We walked out to Fifth Avenue, and we all followed Jonathan. Somehow, things got a little botched up, and Maggie stuck with her friend Diane, while I was with Jonathan. We all paused at the corner and looked back at the church. It was an eerie sight—the bright lights of the TV cameras and the line of people that came out of the darkness and up the steps into the mouth of the cathedral. I thought I might see the end of the line, but it was still nowhere in sight.

As we headed back, Jonathan seemed to be in a good mood again. He was yakking away to me about this and that, and it was just like old times. At first, I didn't really want to listen to him. I still felt down about everything, but soon Jonathan got me out of my mood when he guaranteed to me that the Cardinals were going to win the pennant and the World Series again. He said they were just as good as the Yankees teams of the early sixties. Of course, I said, "No way," and we went on and on comparing the present-day Cardinals to my old Yankees, back when the Yankees were good. After a while, I kind of resented Jonathan for getting me into that conversation because I wanted to spend some more time with Maggie. I knew that could be the last time I ever saw her. I mean, I didn't usually take many trips on my bike to Bloomington. Well, Jonathan wasn't a dummy, and he noticed that I kept glancing back to see how Maggie was doing.

"Yeah, yeah, I know, ole buddy. You've got a crush on Maggie," Jonathan said.

"Hey! No. No way." Of course I had to deny it, but Jonathan knew better.

"Look, T. J., my boy. You've got to play it cool. Don't slobber all over the kid, man. Be cool. She came here with her girlfriend. Don't you think she probably wants to spend a little time with her? And look, there ain't much we can do now. I mean, what do you do after paying your respects to a dead statesman—hit a bar? Go out to dinner? Head down to the Village?"

"Well, I don't know," I said. "I guess you're right."

"Look, T. J., the two chicks are both emotionally drained. They don't recover so fast from these kinds of tragedies."

"Hey, look who's talking," I said. "You wouldn't come out of your house for a week after the Doc was killed."

"Not true," Jonathan said. "I just didn't want to go to school with all you white honkies."

"Oh, so that was it, huh, Jonathan? We're all white honkies. Ha! All white people are responsible for what happened to the Doc. Right?" I was getting really pissed off. I had forgiven Jonathan for not speaking to me for two months, but it made my blood boil when he actually came out and said why. "White honkies, is it? You have to be black to care about somebody like the Doc. Right?"

"Hey now, T. J., let's not get carried away here."

"I suppose Bobby Kennedy was responsible too. Right? And Bobby getting killed was just like the chickens coming home to roost."

"Hey, man, that's not what I mean," Jonathan said, but I was gone before he could finish. I dashed across the street, dodged a few cars, and headed up one of the avenues. I ran as far and as hard as I could, and I didn't know why. Maybe I was just really pissed at Jonathan because he'd left me all alone for two months on the stupid baseball team—two months when I was right in the middle of the big racial mess and when I really needed a friend. Then I stopped. I was tired, and I wasn't mad at Jonathan anymore. I never really had been mad at Jonathan. I knew why he felt the way he did. I understood why some black people blamed white people for the Doc's murder. I knew darn well that some white people were actually happy that Martin Luther King Jr. was dead. I was angry and frustrated that it had to be like that and that someone like Bobby Kennedy, who'd been trying to change it all, had gotten shot too. Would any good ever come of it all? Did people really die in vain?

As I stood there on the corner, Maggie came running up to me.

"Hey, T. J., what's the story?" she asked. "You'd make a heck of a skier with legs like that."

"Yeah," I said. I was real embarrassed this time. "Well, actually, I'm pretty fast around the base paths."

"Oh yeah. You're a baseball player. I forgot," Maggie said. "Oh, Jonathan says he's sorry for what he said. He says he feels like a big jerk. What's with you two anyway? You trying to act like a couple of spoiled toddlers?" We both laughed.

"Nah, I'm not mad at him. I just wanted to stretch my legs a little."

"Oh, I get it. Trying out for the Avenue of the Americas track team." Maggie got me laughing again.

"Yeah, how did you know?" I said, and we headed back. Maggie started telling me stories about a friend of hers who was a track star. I didn't want to ruin her story by telling her that I thought track and field was even more boring than skiing, so I let her go on until we got back to Jonathan and Diane.

We walked the rest of the way back with Jonathan and Diane together in front as Maggie and I followed. Maggie used the track team story to explain why I'd run off like a jerk. We all knew it was just a joke, but at least Maggie saved me from the embarrassment of trying to explain my actions. Jonathan sure as heck knew why I'd run off, and there was no reason to try to explain it to Diane.

I finally knew where we were when we got to Broadway and Forty-Second Street. I hadn't been paying much attention to where we were, but I always knew it when I got to Forty-Second Street, and I sure as heck paid attention when I walked down Forty-Second Street. The crazies were out in full force on that warm spring night, and I felt an obligation to kind of protect Maggie, so I made sure we stayed right behind Jonathan, because whether Jonathan knew it or not, he was protecting me. Maggie grabbed my arm and stayed close.

"This place is a little crazy, but I just love all the people," she said to me. Maggie seemed to have a way to see the positive in things.

When we passed the peep show place Jonathan and I had snuck into, Jonathan looked back and gave me a little wink. *Well, I guess maybe the street has some advantages*, I thought. Jonathan stepped up his pace, and I tried to stay close to him. Jonathan certainly was a master at weaving his way through the screwy pedestrian traffic on Forty-Second Street.

When we got to the bus terminal, everyone was rushing. We all bought our bus tickets, and Maggie and Diane found out that their bus was set to leave in five minutes. Jonathan and I had about a fifteen-minute wait, so we went with the girls as they hurried up to their bus platform. I had no time to think about goodbyes, and Jonathan and I had no time to plot strategy. However, it seemed Maggie had it all figured out. When we got to the escalator, Diane got on, but Maggie stopped short. She opened up her pocketbook, and as fast as she could, she wrote down her phone number on a little piece of paper.

"Come on, Mag!" Diane yelled from halfway up the escalator. "The bus is here!"

"Here, T. J.," Maggie said. "Why don't you call me? Maybe I can see you when school gets out. Our family goes away in the summer, but call me anyway." She started to get on the escalator but stopped.

"Come on, Mag!" Diane called.

Maggie quickly came back to me and gave me a quick kiss and a little hug. "Thanks for putting up with me," she said.

"Oh yeah, but gee." I was too flustered to say anything that made any sense.

"Bye, T. J. Bye, Jonathan," Maggie said as she gave a little wave, and she ran up the escalator. I watched her all the way up. She gave another little wave at the top, and then she was gone.

I walked slowly over to Jonathan. "Come on, lover," he said. I took a swipe at Jonathan for that remark, but he dodged it and ran off with me chasing him. When I caught him, I gave him a big shove, and then we both started laughing.

# CHAPTER 14

# Darrell's Demise

It wasn't Darrell who exploded. It was the coach, and it happened during the last game of the season. The game was at Roosevelt Field against Cliffside. In the first inning, Darrell hit one of the longest balls I'd ever seen any high school kid hit. There was nobody on base, and Darrell, being the hot dog that he was, stood at home plate and watched the ball sail out there as if he were Hank Aaron watching a home run sail over the fence. The trouble was, there were no fences at Roosevelt Field. Every ball was in play no matter how far it went, and once Darrell started running, he could see that the center fielder for Cliffside wasn't going to allow the hit to be an automatic home run. After jogging to first base in his Hank Aaron home run trot, Darrell must have figured he'd better start moving his behind. Darrell had never been known for his speed, but he made it all the way around to third, and Jonathan, who was coaching third, gave Darrell the green light to head for home. However, for some reason, Darrell stopped just as he rounded third. Well, the center fielder, who had made a pretty darn good play, threw the ball to the shortstop. The shortstop was out in short center field and was about to make the long relay throw to the plate. It would have taken a perfect throw to get even someone with Darrell's lack of speed. That was why Jonathan was waving Darrell in, and everybody was expecting a close play at the plate. Well, since Darrell stopped dead, there was no play at the plate, but the shortstop's throw was so lousy that it bounced about fifteen times and was ten feet off target. The ball rattled around the backstop for about ten minutes before the catcher could get ahold of it. All the while, Darrell stood with his tongue out, panting, at third base with one of the longest triples anybody had ever seen. Needless to say, the coach wasn't too happy, and of course, the coach was not one to keep his feelings inside. When the next batter popped out stranding Darrell at third, the coach really blasted Darrell. We could all see that Darrell did not appreciate the coach's tirade.

As per usual for Darrell, after hitting his mighty long ball his first time up, his next two times up, he tried to hit the ball even farther but struck out, stranding a runner both times. We could see that the coach was fuming.

It was a close game, 3–3, and we needed a few big hits. We also needed to play some good defense. Well, Darrell had made an error earlier in the game that caused a run, and the error he made in the top of the sixth inning caused more than a few runs for Cliffside. There were two out and two on for Cliffside, and one of their weakest hitters was up. The guy hit a high pop to short left field, and Darrell immediately waved everybody off. He waved his arms, yelling, "I've got it! I've got it!" However, he wasn't hustling too much. He was just slowly and casually backpedaling. He never did get under the ball; instead, he stuck up his glove in an effort to make a one-handed grab, but the ball bounced off his glove and bounded away. Darrell lost his balance and then did a backward somersault.

While Darrell was tumbling around, our left fielder chased after the ball, but by the time he got the ball back to the infield, the Cliffside batter was all the way around to third base with one of the all-time shortest triples anyone had ever seen, and two runs had scored. Now, all that was nothing compared to what Darrell did next. While getting up from his backward somersault, Darrell started laughing—not loudly, but he was chuckling with a big grin on his face. He didn't want to act like he was embarrassed for looking like such a fool and allowing two runs to score, so he figured it would be cool to laugh at himself. Well, the coach did not think Darrell's effort on the play was funny. When the coach saw Darrell grinning after just about single-handedly blowing the whole game, the coach went bananas. He ran out onto the field, screaming at Darrell.

"What are you grinning about? That was the worst frigging play I've ever seen in my life! And what the heck are you laughing about?" The coach was yelling so loudly that the veins were popping out of his neck.

"Hey, man, lay off," Darrell said, but he wasn't smiling anymore.

"Get off the field, boy!" the coach yelled with his neck veins popping and his face red.

"Hey, man, don't call me boy," Darrell said, trying to stay cool.

"I'll call you whatever I darn well please, boy! Now, get off this field! This field is for ballplayers, not little boys who giggle like you."

"Hey, man, lay off," Darrell said as he stood his ground.

"I said get off the field! And for that matter, get off the team!"

Then Darrell lit the fuse—and the coach did not have a long one. Darrell said calmly, "Make me, sucker."

*Kaboom!* One coach totally detonated!

The coach jumped on Darrell and wrestled him to the ground. The umpire was the first to get over there to try to break up the fight, but everybody on our team went over to join in. Then the other team's bench emptied, and we had a full-scale major-league rhubarb. Of course, we weren't mad at anybody from the other team, and they weren't mad at us, so we really didn't have anybody to fight. In a major-league rhubarb, nobody really fought either. The players just liked to roll around in the grass for a while to give the fans a show. Luckily, the umpire was a big bruiser, and he was able to stop the fight quickly. He gave both the coach and Darrell the heave-ho. He ordered Darrell to leave the field and head home, and he made the coach go sit in his car by the garbage trucks until the end of the game. Since it was the last game of the season for us kids, the umpire decided to let us play the last innings, and he appointed Jonathan as coach. Unsurprisingly, Jonathan relished his new role.

His first managerial move after the commotion died down was to send me out to shortstop. It was a move that Jonathan would later boast was brilliant, even though it was pretty academic because I was the only other shortstop on the team. Well, the next guy up for Cliffside hit a grounder up the middle. I was able to scoot over to grab it, and I made a perfect sidearm off-balance throw to first to nip the runner and save a run. Happily, the coach wasn't around to complain about my sidearm throw.

We scraped together a run in the bottom of the sixth and shut out Cliffside in the top of the seventh, so we were down by only a run in the bottom of the seventh. We had two out and a man on first when Gorski came up. I was on deck. I hoped to get a crack at knocking in the winning run, but the pitcher was a tough righty with a good curveball. He didn't have much speed, but a good curveball was my nemesis. Well, Gorski looked as if he were going to solve everything when he hit a long shot up the left-center field gap that looked like a sure home run. We were all screaming like crazy for Gorski to come all the way around, but Gorski was no speed demon, and Jonathan, who was coaching third in addition to managing, held Gorski up at third. It was another brilliant move, Jonathan would later claim. I had to admit he was right because the throw home that time, unlike on Darrell's play, was by the right fielder, who had a great arm and had come all the way over for the cutoff.

His throw to the plate was perfect and surely would have made Gorski a dead duck.

Now was my chance. I had hardly played in two weeks, and there I was, at bat with the winning run on third and two out in the last inning of the last game of the season, facing a big righty pitcher with a good curveball.

As I was just about to settle into the batter's box, I heard Jonathan call my name. He was coming toward me. I asked the umpire for time and went over to Jonathan for a little conference. It was like the last game of the World Series, and it was as if Frankie Crosetti were telling Bobby Richardson some great strategy, such as "I know you've only hit two home runs in six hundred at bats this year, Richardson, but we could sure use one now." However, I underestimated ole Jonathan. I had to admit that in all the confusion, I never would have even tried it. But I did exactly what Jonathan told me: I got up lefty for the first time all year, and on the first pitch, I laid down a perfect drag bunt.

I got it by the pitcher, and since the second baseman and first baseman were playing back, never expecting a two-out bunt, they were surprised, and I beat it out easily. Gorski rumbled down the line, jumped on home plate, and we won! We all went wild! It was as if we had just won the World Series. It was quite a way to end the season, and of course, I knew I'd never hear the end of it from Jonathan about his brilliant strategy.

# CHAPTER 15

# Mickey Mantle's Last Home Run

I got off the bus at the Port Authority around seven o'clock and headed down to the subways. I took the A train to Fifty-Ninth Street and the D train right on up to the stadium. One could always tell what train to take just by watching out for families with little squirts carrying baseball gloves and trailing after their fathers. Of course, one never could be sure if those fathers knew their way around the subways, but I was pretty sure of my way, having made the trip several times with Jonathan. I kind of missed having Jonathan around to follow.

Seeing little squirts with gloves reminded me of the times my father had taken my brother and me to the stadium. Of course, my father always went by car. I didn't think he'd like to take his little kids down into these grimy subways.

I made it to the stadium in good time. I bought my general admission ticket and headed to the upper deck.

I loved the smell of the old ballpark—kind of like cigars mixed with peanuts. It was a small crowd. After all, when a team was out of the pennant race in September, not many people felt like coming out, so I got a good seat behind home plate. I debated whether I should go down toward first base to be closer to the Mick, but I decided to stay behind home since that was where I'd told Jonathan I'd be. The game's start was pretty boring, and the Red Sox got off to a one-run lead. I hated the Red Sox.

The Mick came up in the bottom of the third against Jim Lonborg and got a big ovation. He got a big ovation those days no matter what he did. Every time they announced his name, people cheered, and when he came to bat, he always got a standing ovation. I knew the Mick was great—he'd always been great—but heck, what was the big deal? I thought a lot of fans felt guilty because they used to boo the Mick in his younger days, even though he was hitting at least forty home runs every year. I thought they were all trying to apologize to the Mick now, and that was okay with me. *And they'll have plenty of time to keep apologizing next year and the year after that and probably the year after that!* I thought.

After the cheers died down, it didn't take long for the Mick to connect. He sent a long, low line drive that sailed deep into the lower right-field stands for his eighteenth home run of the year. He got another standing ovation as he trotted around the bases. I stood up, but I always did when the Mick hit one out. It was no big deal, actually. Now, when Horace Clarke hit a home run, *that* was a big deal!

However, as I watched the Mick circle the bases, all of a sudden, I felt a terrible pang of sadness. I couldn't understand it. It was almost like the sadness I'd felt the morning I'd heard that Bobby Kennedy had been shot. The Mick looked tired as he went around the bases. Everybody knew he didn't run well anymore with his banged-up knees, but he seemed to go around the bases especially slowly. He still bounced his shoulders with his elbows up, but even that seemed pained, like the movement of an old man. As the Mick crossed the plate, everybody continued standing and cheering, but I had to sit down. The scene was too sad. I didn't know why, but I felt really sad.

Just then, I felt a poke in my back. I turned around and saw a big black face with a ridiculous Groucho Marx disguise on, wearing a red St. Louis Cardinals cap and chomping on a big cigar.

"Jonathan! You maniac!" I said, cracking up. "Take that stupid disguise off."

"Why? Are there any Golgi bodies around?" Jonathan said, and then he cracked up too. He took the mask off and sat down beside me. "Well, T. J., buddy, have a cigar, why don't you?"

"What?" I said.

"Have a cigar to celebrate Mickey Mantle's five hundred thirty-sixth home run."

"You're crazy, Jonathan," I said.

"Well, let me put it this way. I'm starting a new club. It's called the sentence club. You see, all you have to do is smoke a cigar while wearing a Groucho Marx disguise and a St. Louis Cardinals cap, and you can be admitted to the sentence as a preposition. Just think how it could liven up Miss Stewart's eleventh-grade English class."

"You *are* a maniac," I said. I gave Jonathan a shove, and he almost fell out of his seat. "Gimme a cigar."

"Now you're talking," Jonathan said.

I'd always thought it would be pretty cool to smoke a cigar.

"Smoking a cigar will get you into the sentence but only as a past participle," Jonathan said.

"I'll take it," I said. Jonathan lit my cigar.

"Here's to number five-thirty-six for the Mick. May there be many more. And, T. J., my boy, welcome to the sentence."

"Sounds good to me," I said, and we sat back to enjoy the game.

**Steven A. Falco** grew up playing baseball in the New Jersey suburbs of New York City. He majored in English at Montclair State University where he studied Steinbeck, Dylan, and Berra. Falco worked for many years in social services and continues to play ball. He is the author of *Grandpa Gordy's Greatest World Series Games.*